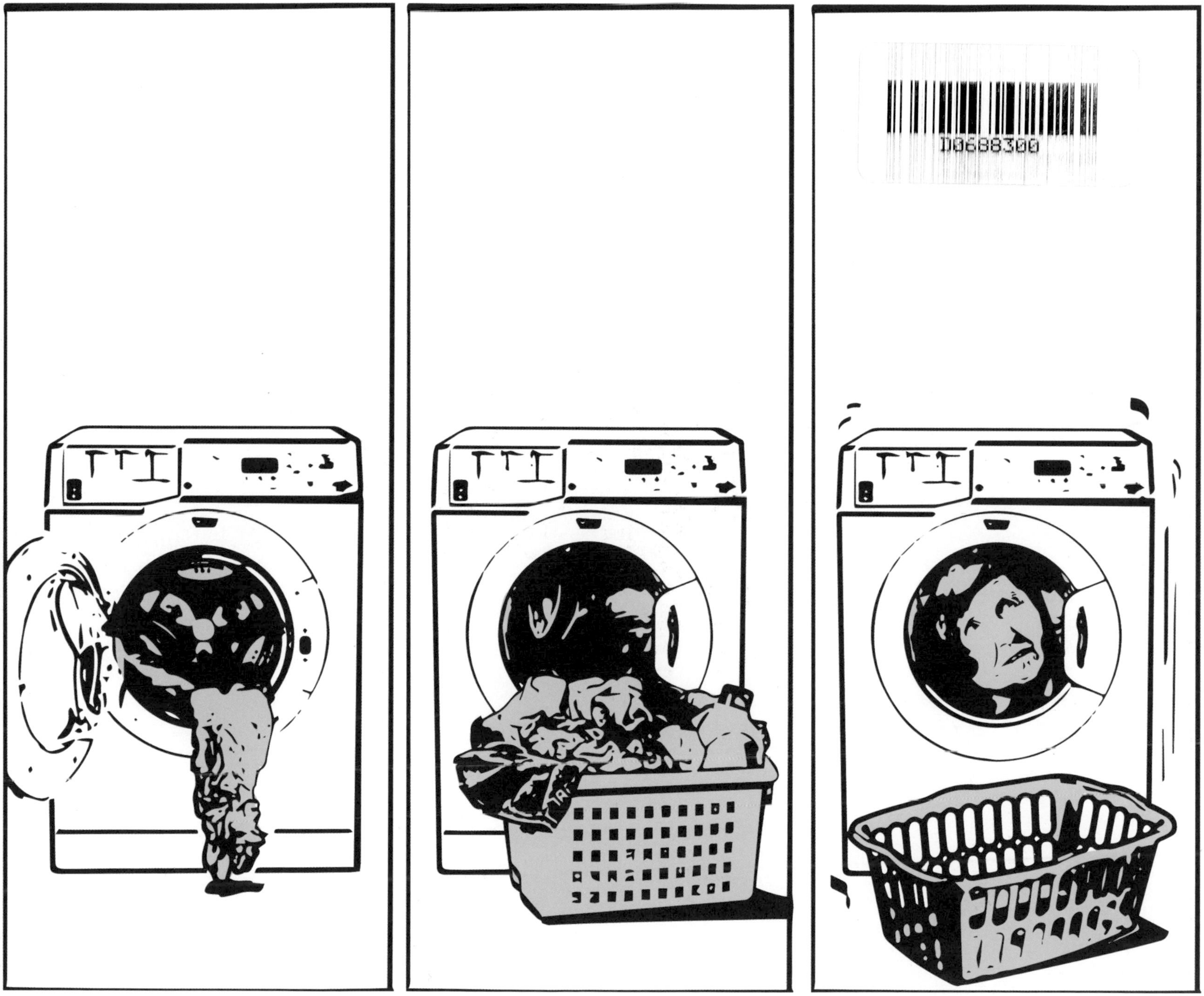

The Courage of Elfina

Text by **André Jacob**
Illustrated by **Christine Delezenne**
Translated by **Susan Ouriou**

James Lorimer & Company Ltd., Publishers
Toronto

The Courage of Elfina

Text by **André Jacob**
Illustrated by **Christine Delezenne**
Translated by **Susan Ouriou**

Prologue

Not a day goes by that I don't go back there in my mind.
It's like I've been adrift for a long time,
huddled in the bottom of a dugout canoe,
not knowing where I'll land. I was eight
when Mama Eva died giving birth
to my little brother. Papá was away, as usual,
because he worked on a big farm over in Brazil.
Grandma and a neighbour helped her as best they could,
but they couldn't save her.
My brother and I stayed on at home.
I kept going to the little village school
and helping Grandma. I adore her.
She's a real miracle worker. She sings as she cooks
and heals our nicks and scrapes with
medicine she concocts using plants.

I'd just turned twelve and
was sitting with Grandma under
the giant mango tree that lords over our yard
when she told me some news
I could barely take in:
Aunt Evoala, one of my dad's sisters,
had invited me to live
with her in Asunción,
the capital of my country,
Paraguay.

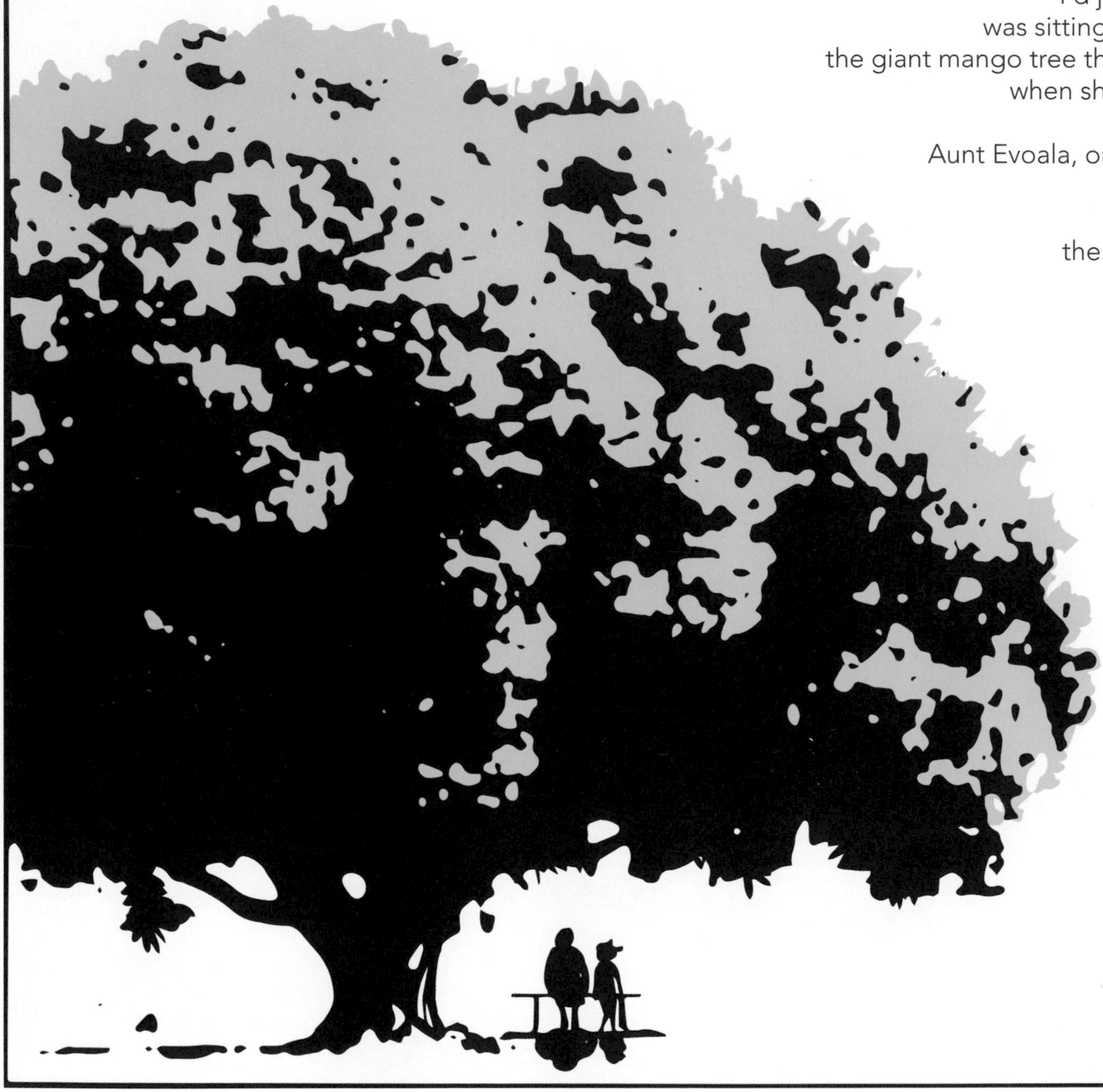

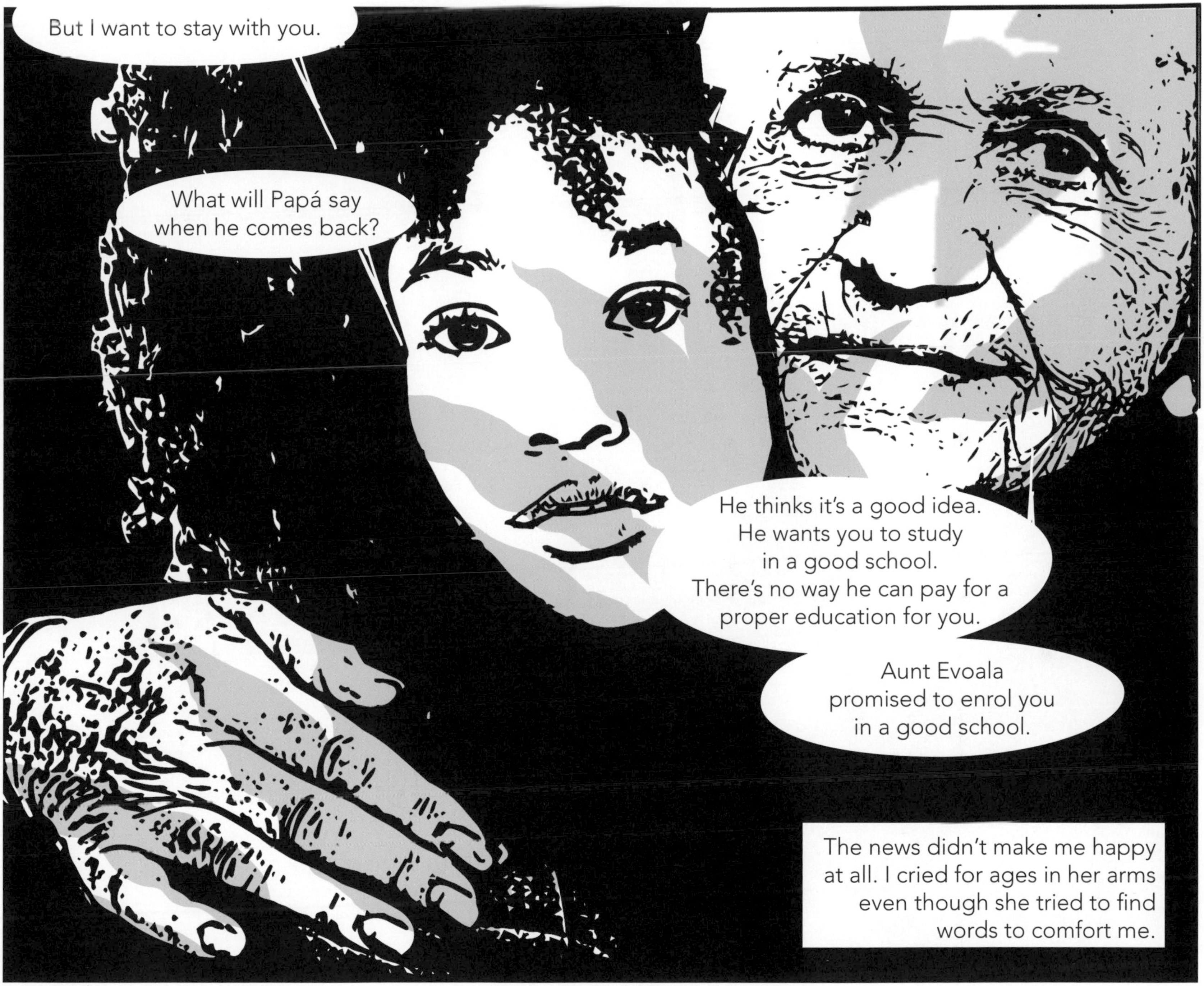
But I want to stay with you.
What will Papá say when he comes back?
He thinks it's a good idea. He wants you to study in a good school. There's no way he can pay for a proper education for you.
Aunt Evoala promised to enrol you in a good school.
The news didn't make me happy at all. I cried for ages in her arms even though she tried to find words to comfort me.

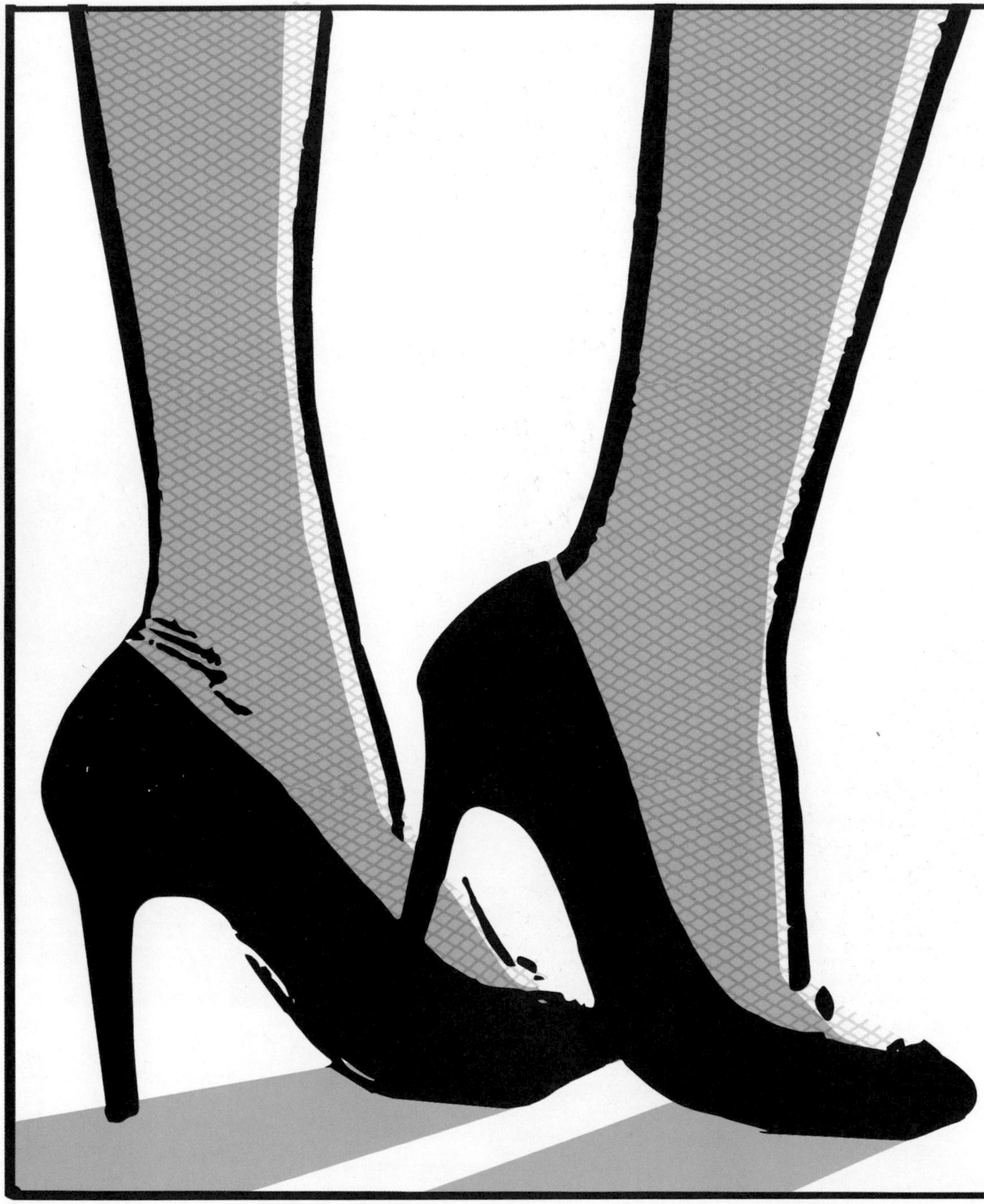

A few days later,
I left my village on
the banks of the great Paraguay
River. On the bus taking
me to the capital,
I felt lost and sad.
I had never met
Aunt Evoala.
When I arrived, after travelling
hundreds of kilometres,
a woman walked up
to me.

Hello!

Are you Elfina?

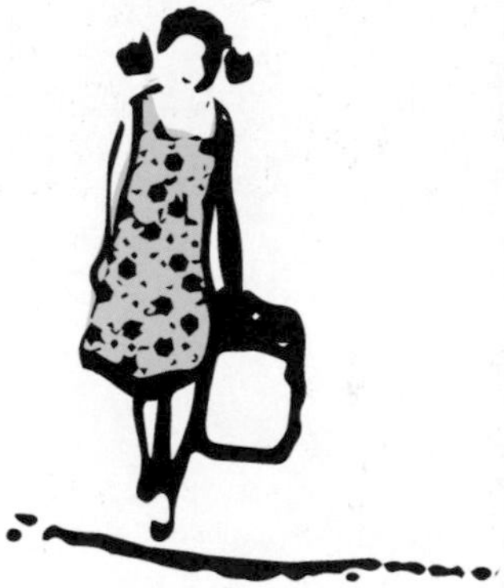

Yes, I mumbled,
my eyes riveted on her
shoes as red and shiny
as pomegranates.

Aunt Evoala didn't add a single word. Not another sound crossed my lips. Her cold stare, her bright red lipstick, her gold jewellery, and her long black dress all intimidated me. She gestured for me to climb into the back seat of her car.

My heart ached during the whole drive. When we pulled up to her house, it was like coming to a real live castle.

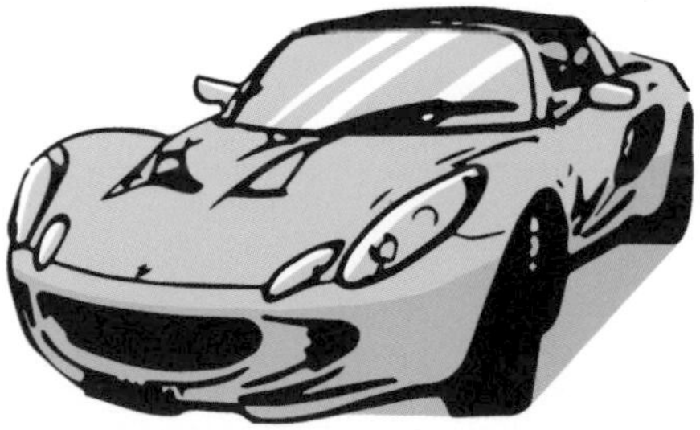

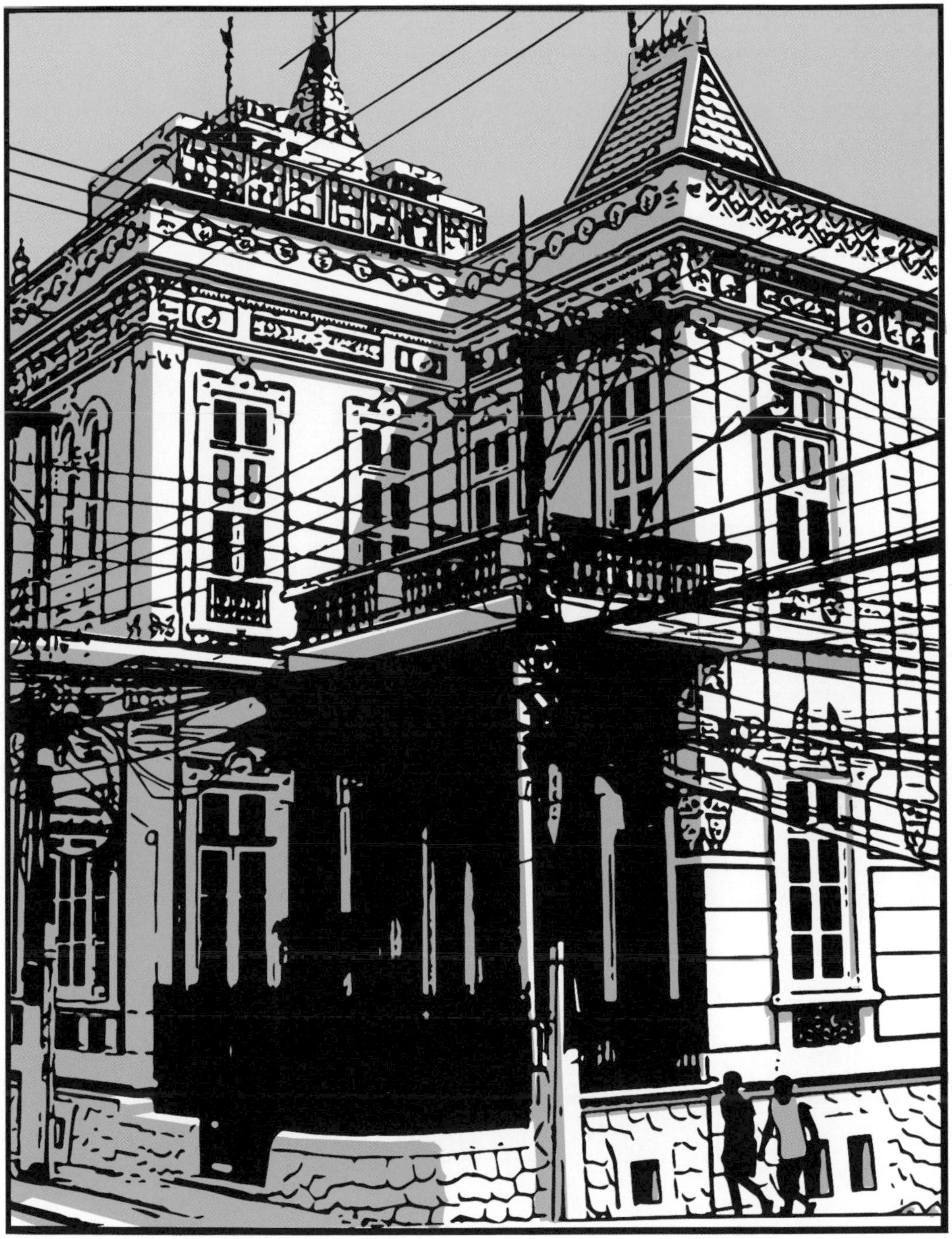

As soon as we stepped inside, my aunt
took me to a tiny bedroom built above
the garage and gave me her first order:
Put your things away and come down
to the kitchen!

I sat on the edge
of my cot, not moving
for the longest time,

a prisoner,
like a goldfish in a bowl.

I felt totally
out of my element.

In the kitchen, Aunt Evoala introduced me to my cousins Fabri and Hector. Eyes glued to the TV, they said hi and nothing more.

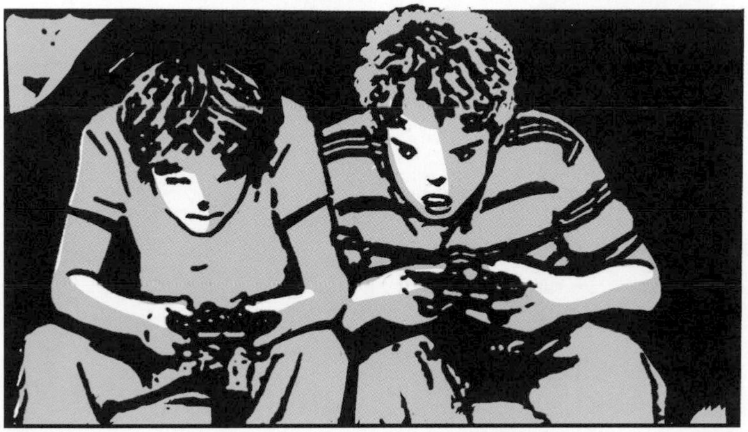

As for my other cousin, even though she kept tapping on her phone, she did walk up to me with a smile.

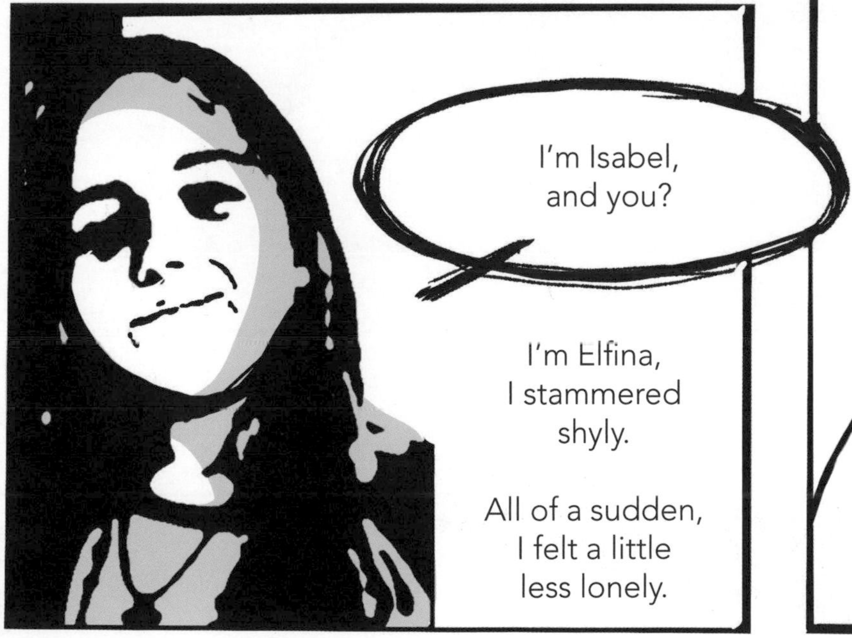
I'm Isabel, and you?
I'm Elfina, I stammered shyly.
All of a sudden, I felt a little less lonely.

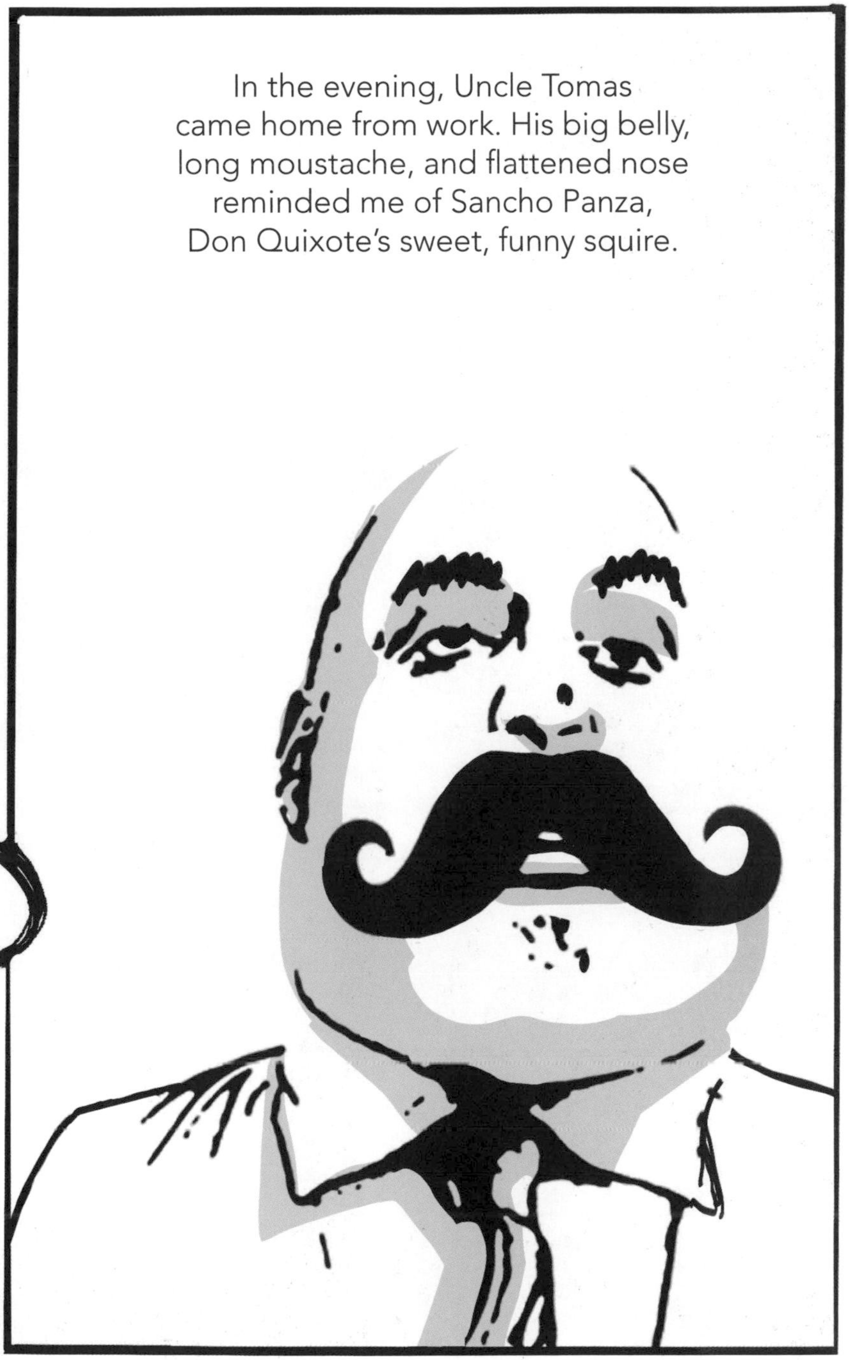
In the evening, Uncle Tomas came home from work. His big belly, long moustache, and flattened nose reminded me of Sancho Panza, Don Quixote's sweet, funny squire.

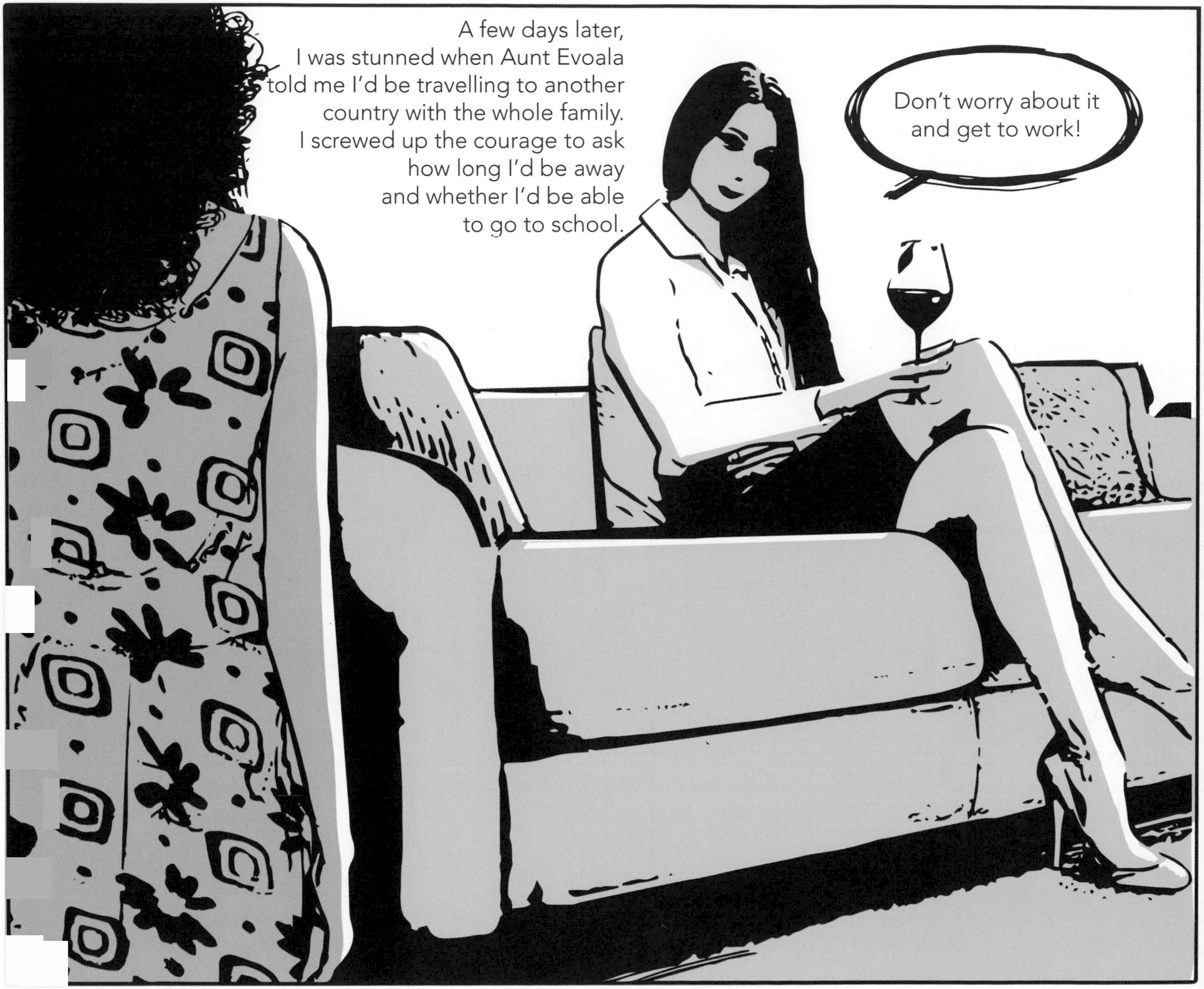
A few days later, I was stunned when Aunt Evoala told me I'd be travelling to another country with the whole family. I screwed up the courage to ask how long I'd be away and whether I'd be able to go to school.
Don't worry about it and get to work!

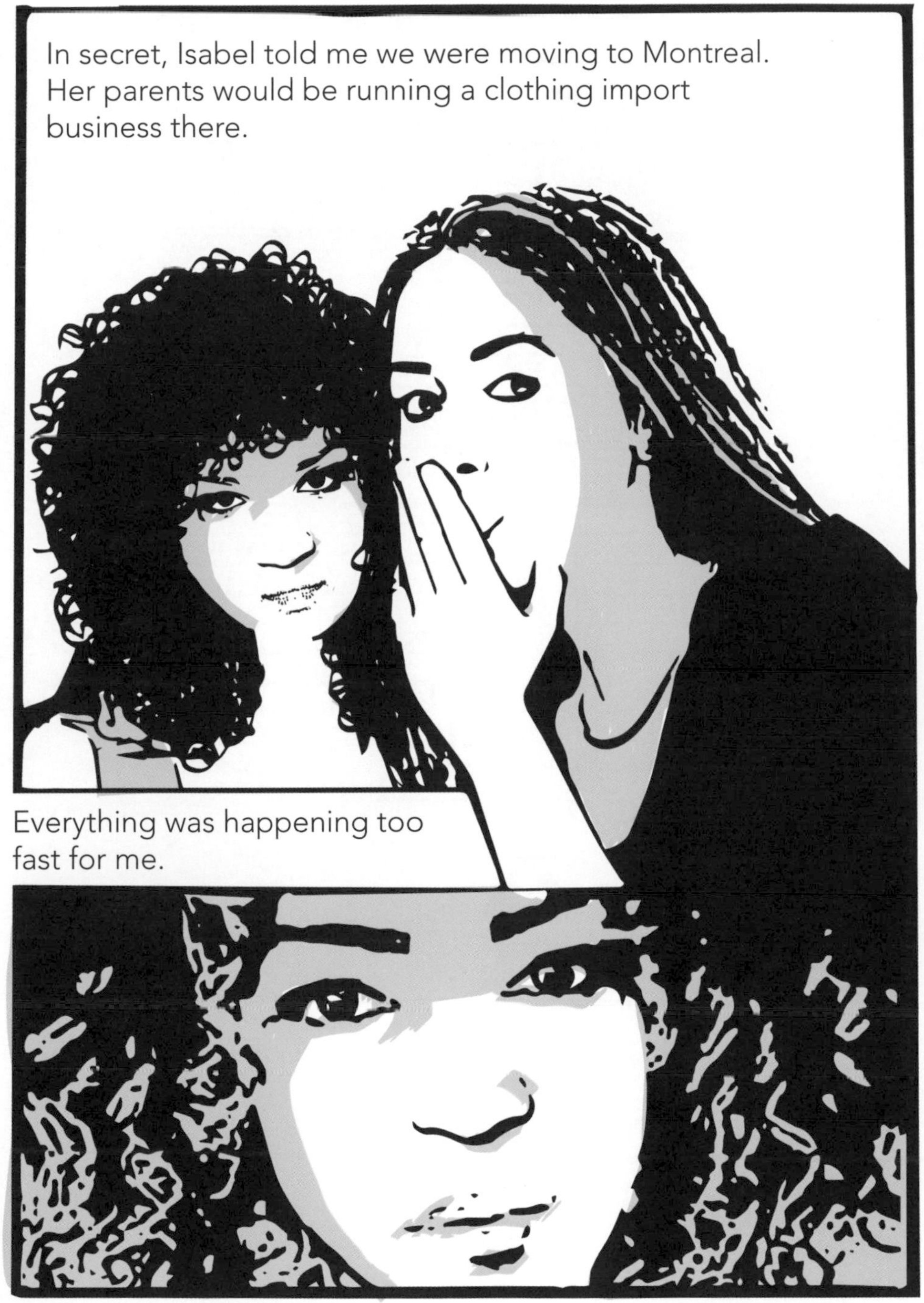
In secret, Isabel told me we were moving to Montreal. Her parents would be running a clothing import business there.
Everything was happening too fast for me.

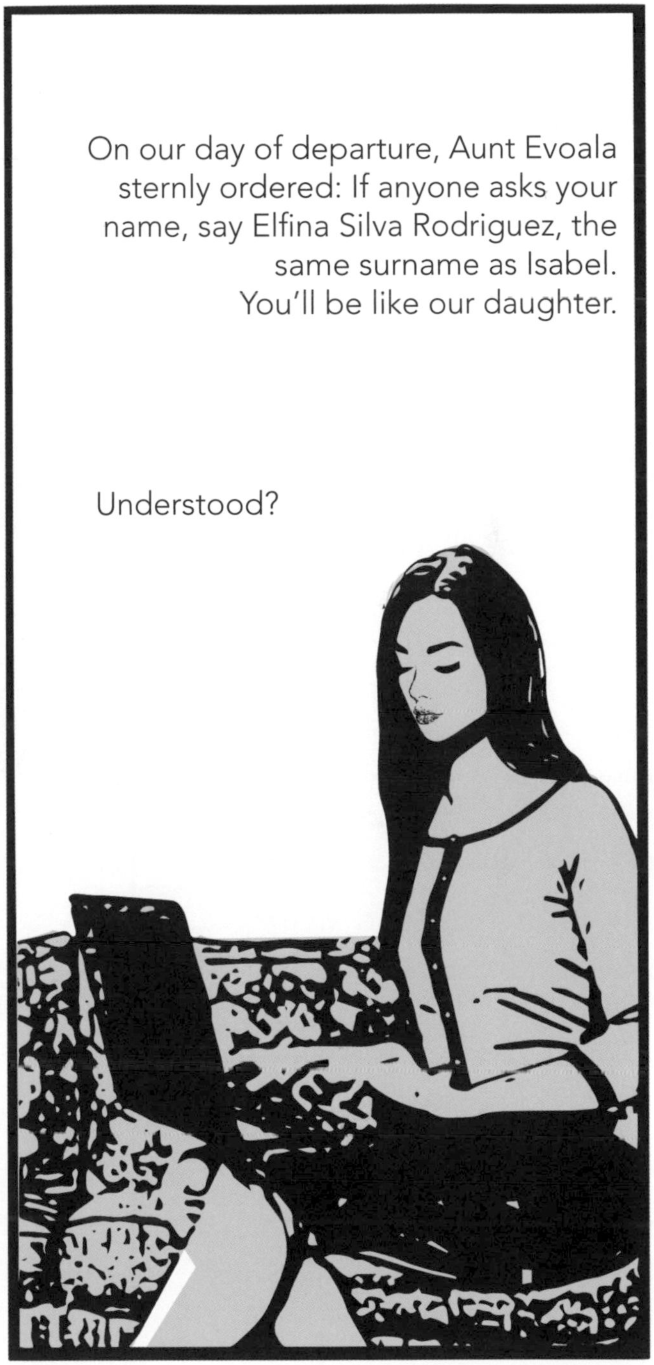
On our day of departure, Aunt Evoala sternly ordered: If anyone asks your name, say Elfina Silva Rodriguez, the same surname as Isabel. You'll be like our daughter.
Understood?

When it came time to get on the plane, I did as Aunt Evoala ordered. I walked on board like a robot, not knowing what lay ahead.

My eyes brimming with tears,

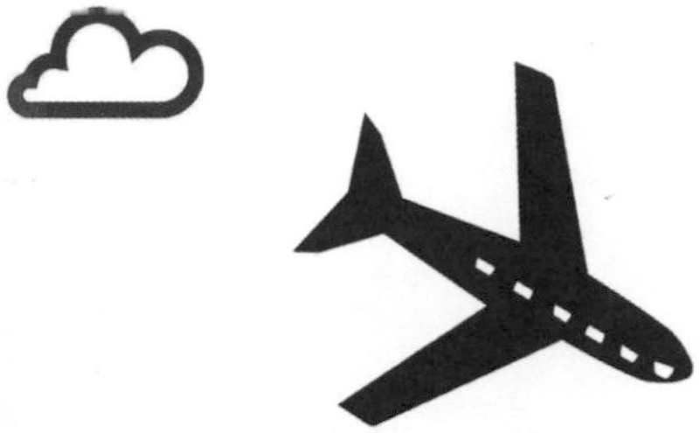

I felt my past fading away.

When we arrived in Montreal, I followed, as silent as a stone. A driver dropped us off in front of a big house at the end of an avenue lined with giant trees.

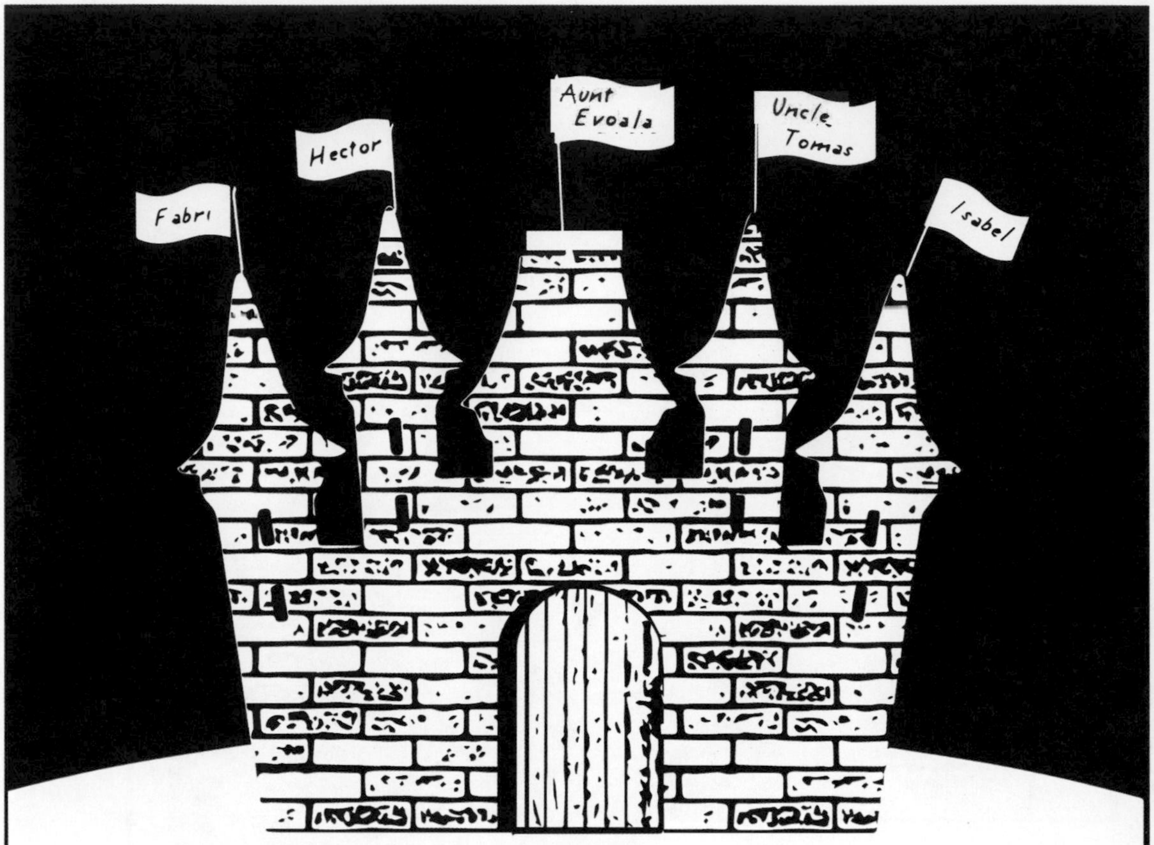
Fabri
Hector
Aunt Evoala
Uncle Tomas
Isabel

The red-brick turret, big windows, and high walls could have made me believe I was about to enter Cinderella's castle,

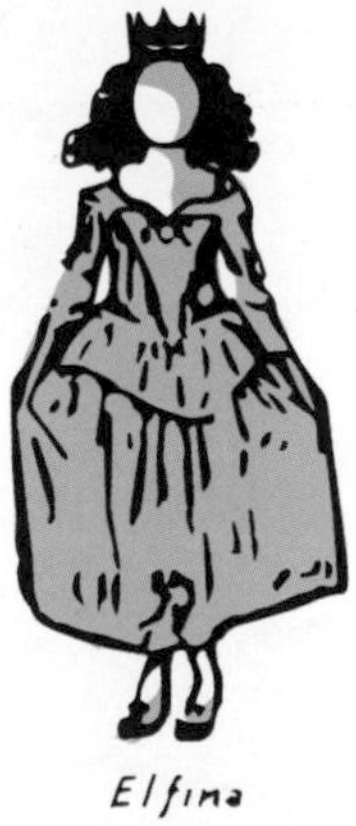
Elfina

but I was in no mood for daydreaming.

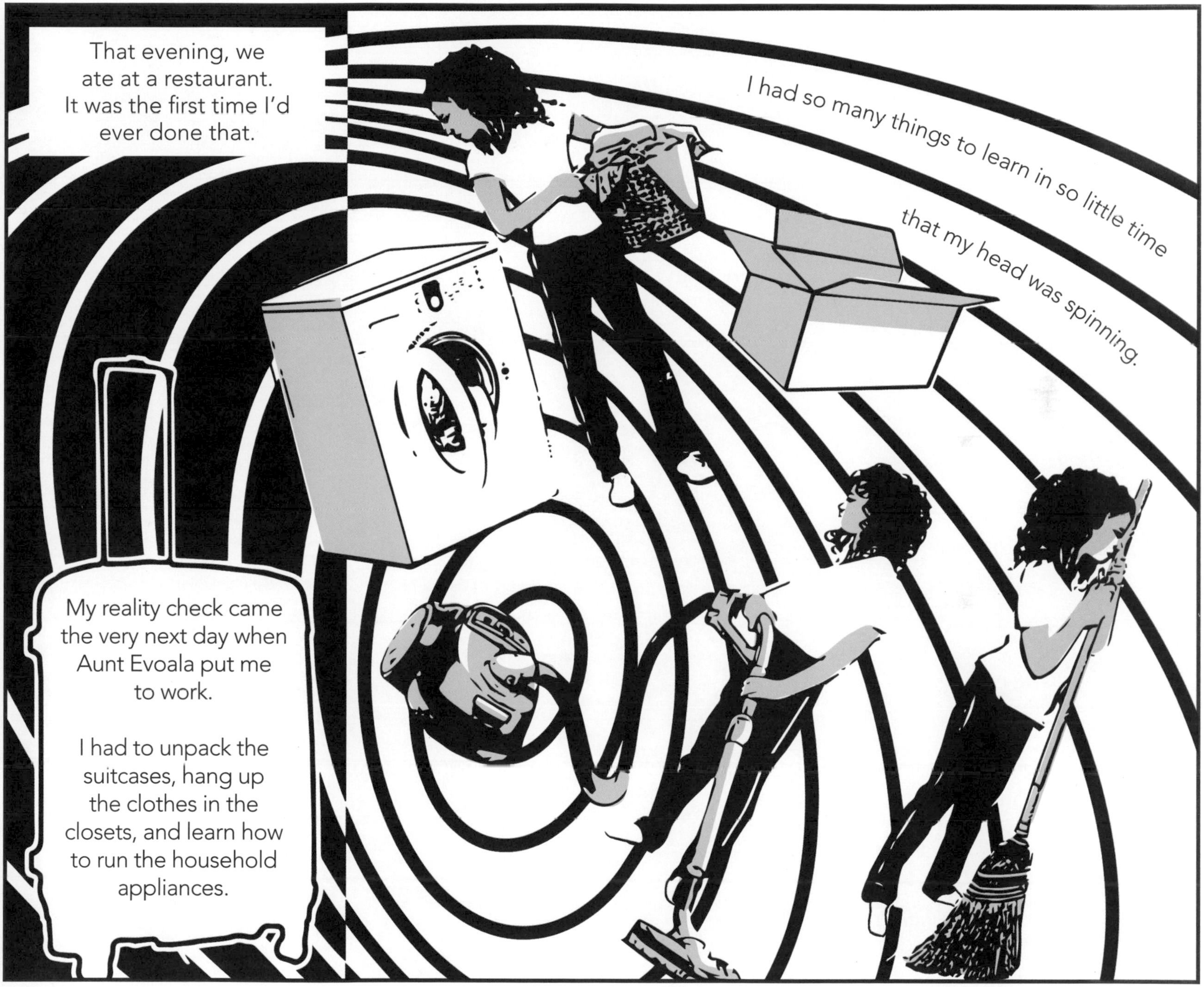

That evening, we ate at a restaurant. It was the first time I'd ever done that.
I had so many things to learn in so little time
that my head was spinning.
My reality check came the very next day when Aunt Evoala put me to work.
I had to unpack the suitcases, hang up the clothes in the closets, and learn how to run the household appliances.

Fall

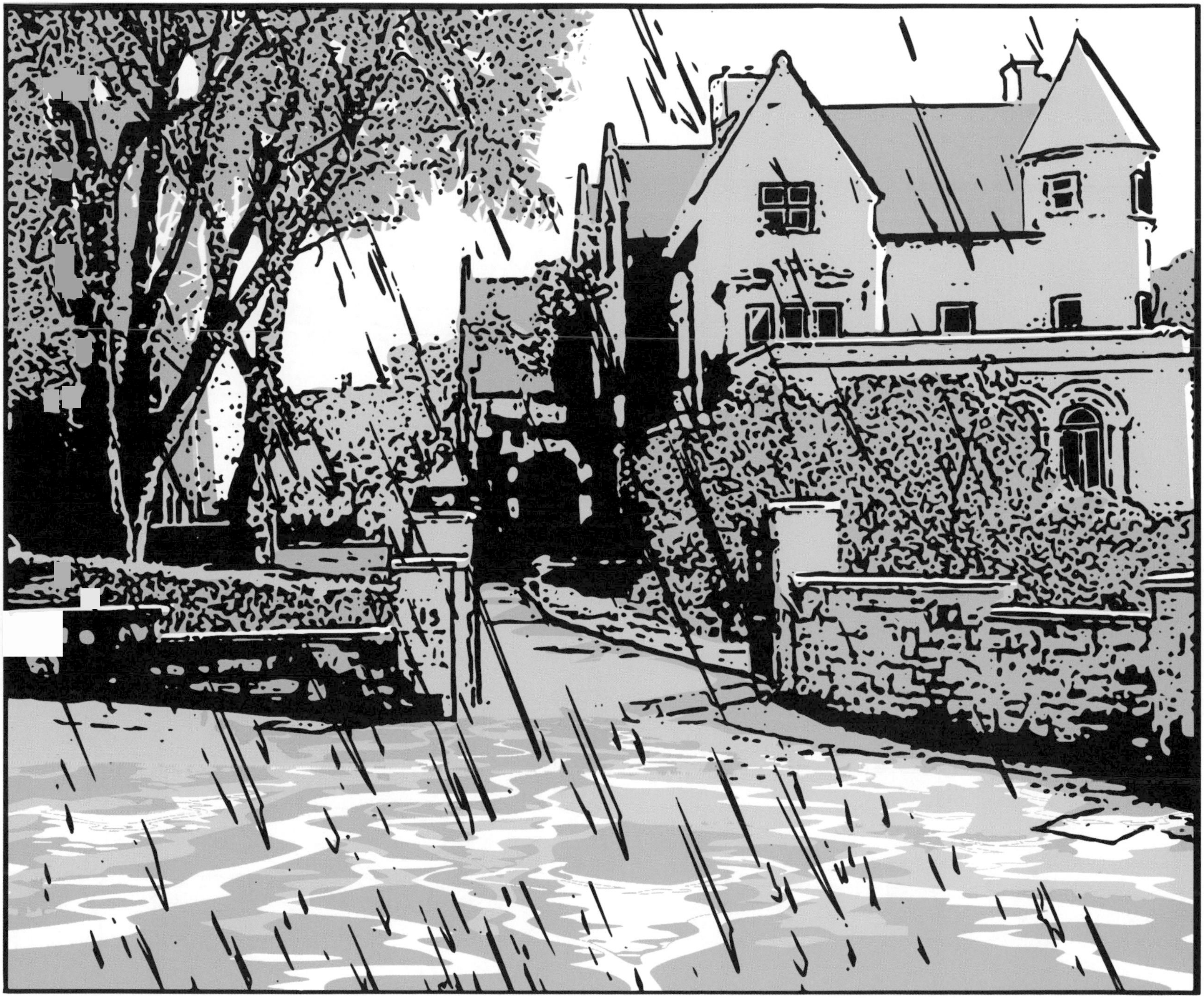

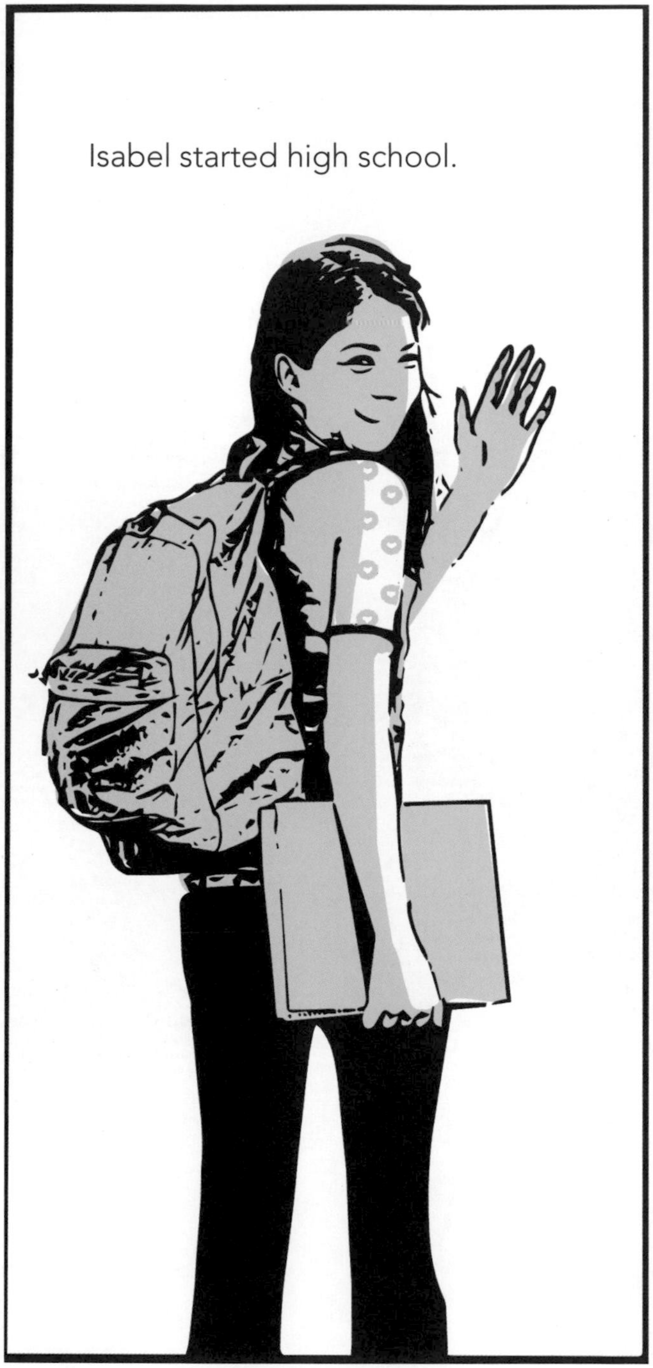
Isabel started high school.

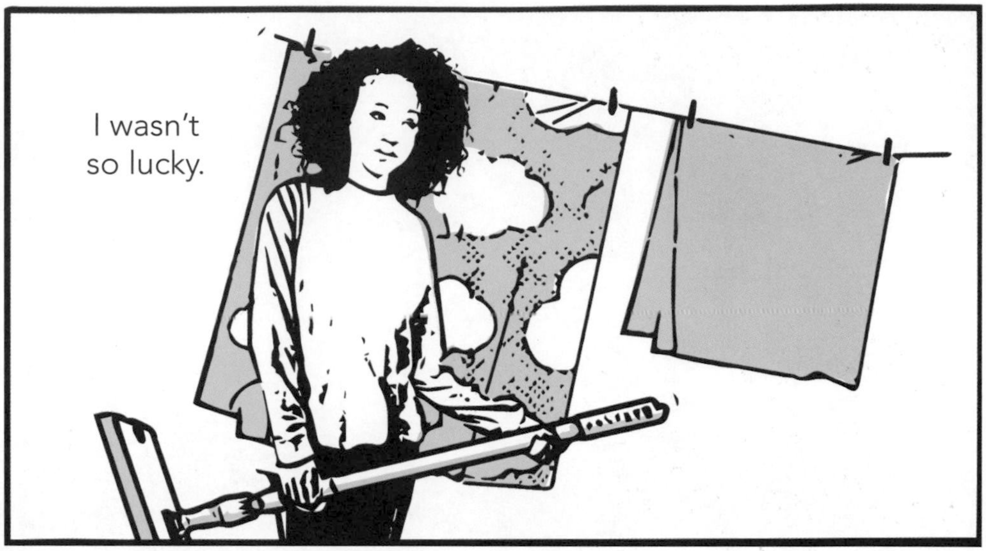
I wasn't
so lucky.

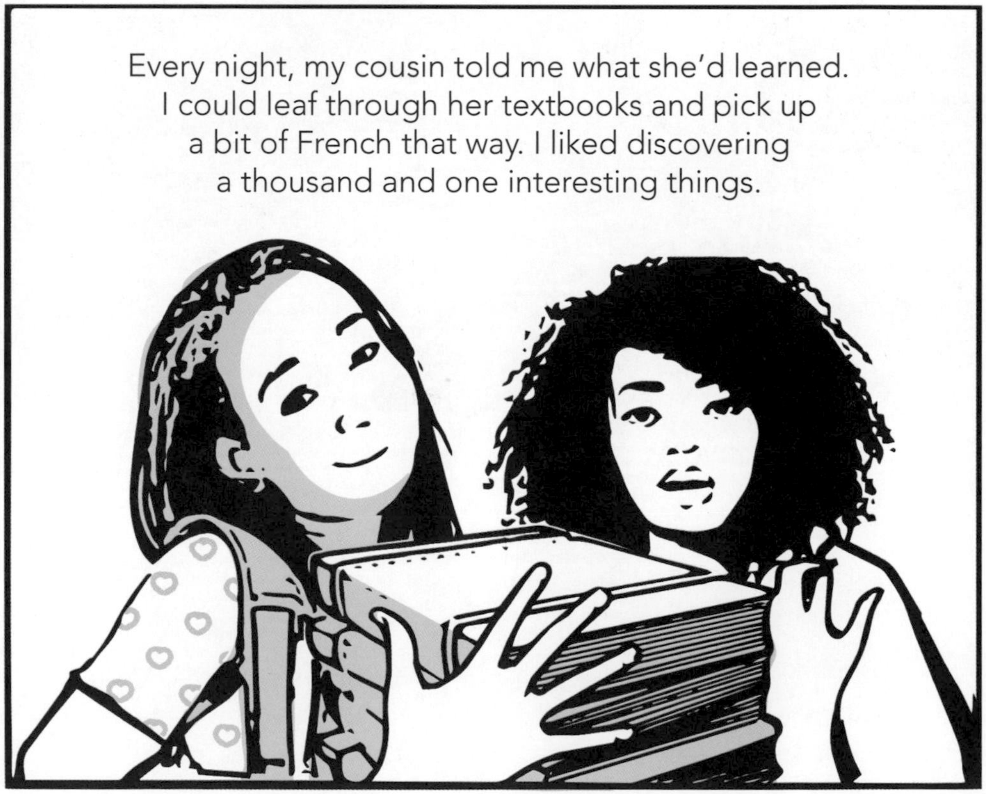
Every night, my cousin told me what she'd learned.
I could leaf through her textbooks and pick up
a bit of French that way. I liked discovering
a thousand and one interesting things.

Fabri and Hector
weren't interested in me,
except when they wanted me to do
something for them,

like iron a shirt.

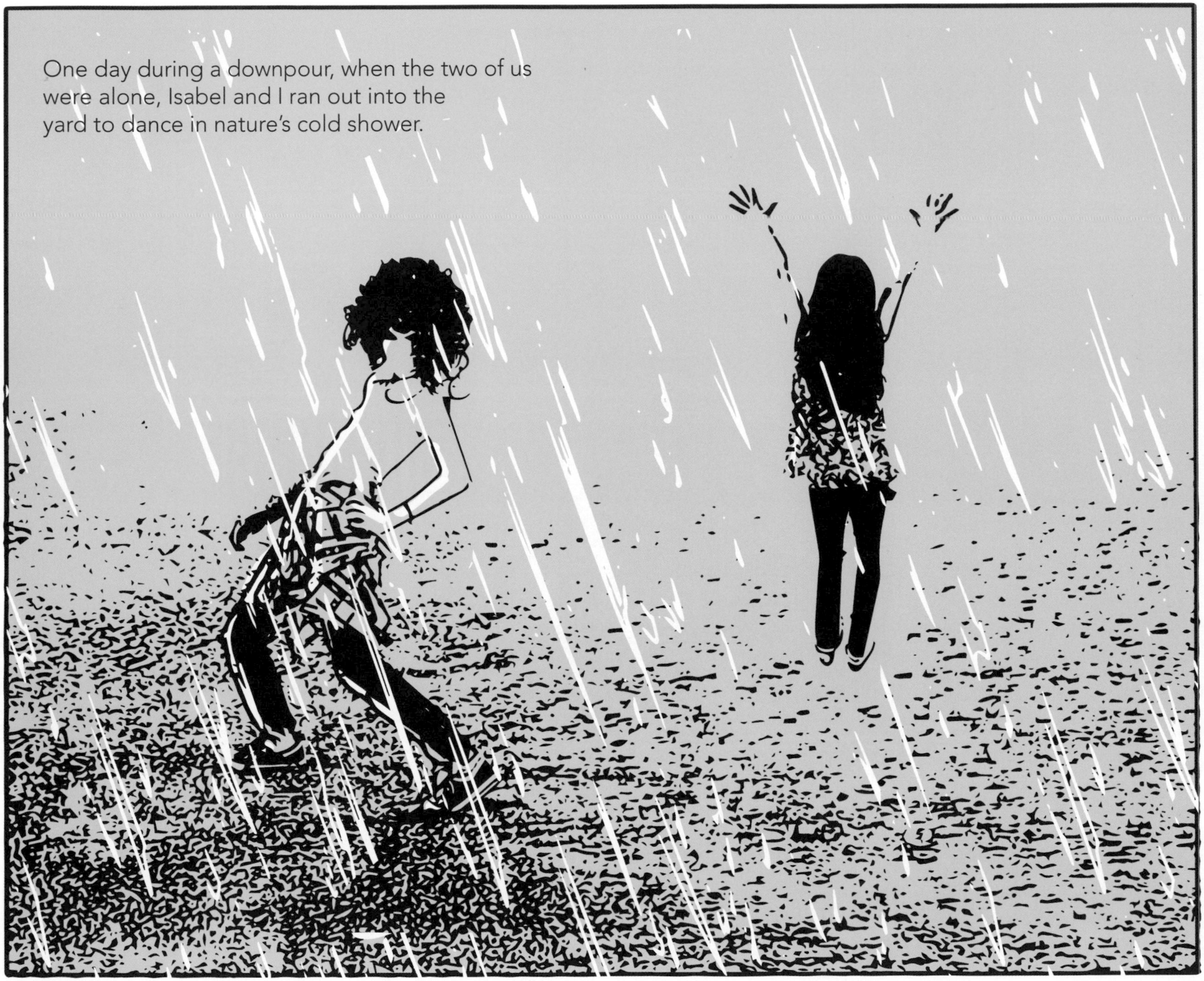
One day during a downpour, when the two of us were alone, Isabel and I ran out into the yard to dance in nature's cold shower.

We looked like two lunatics at a witches' dance party.
We spun around and around, clapping our hands
and singing at the top of our lungs.
After we fell dizzily to the grass,
we stood up again to dry off our clothes
and get back to work.

Isabel to her homework

and me to the pots and pans.

The chauffeur
soon taught me
to do the shopping.

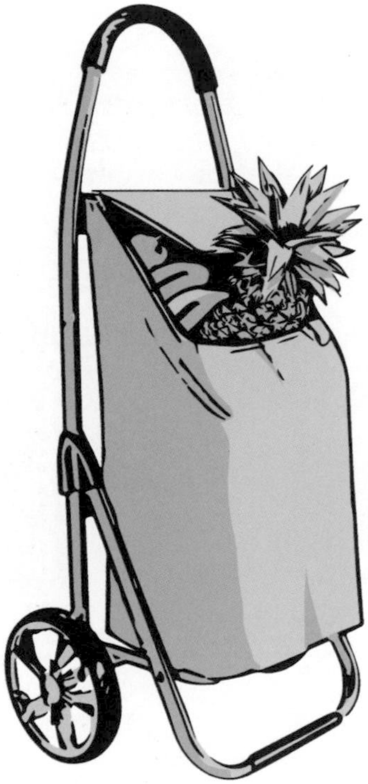

I was fascinated by all the displays
overflowing with glorious fruits
and vegetables of every colour.

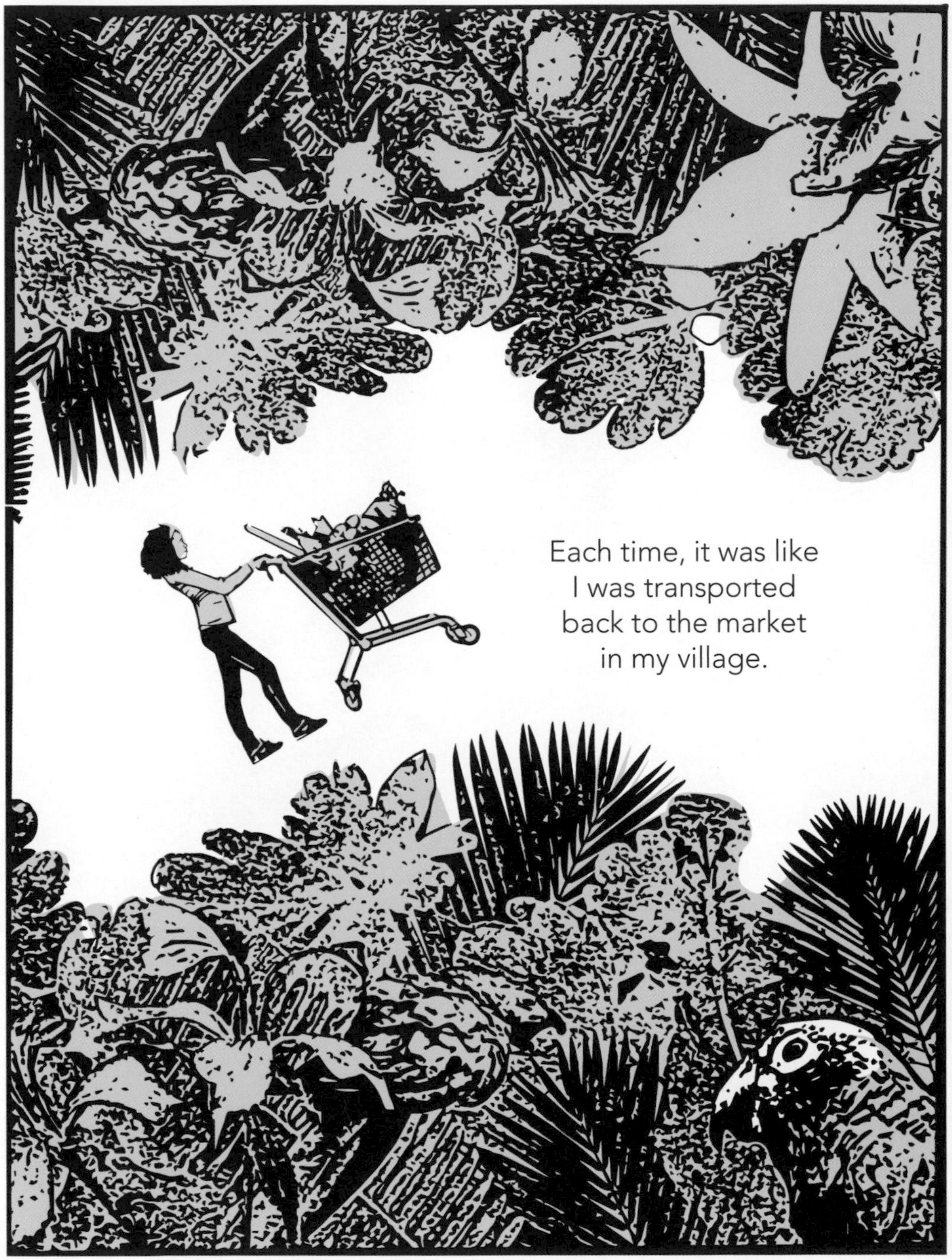
Each time, it was like
I was transported
back to the market
in my village.

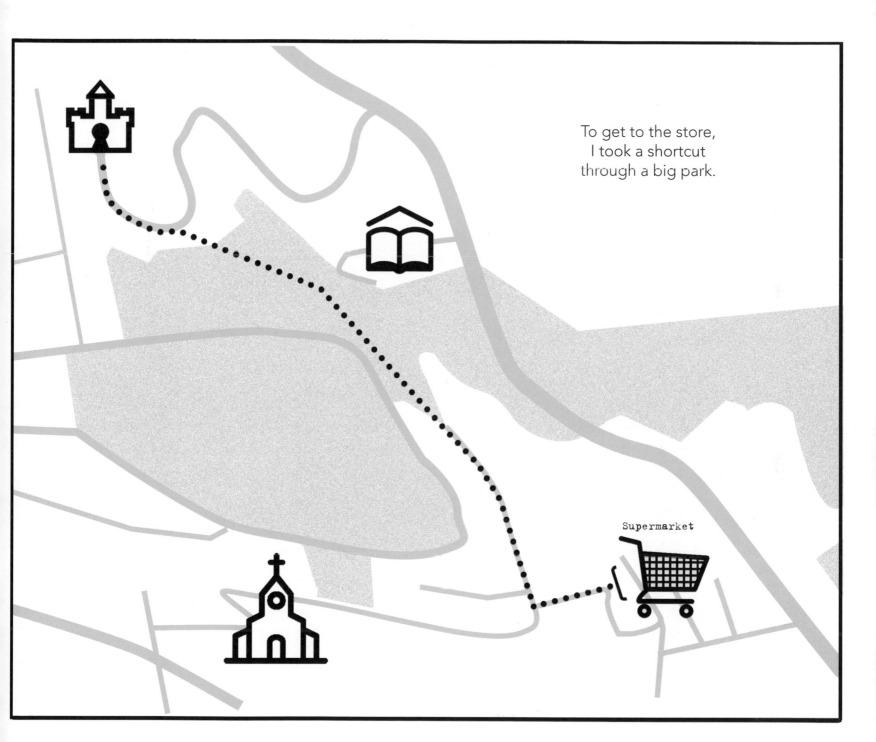

To get to the store,
I took a shortcut
through a big park.

Supermarket

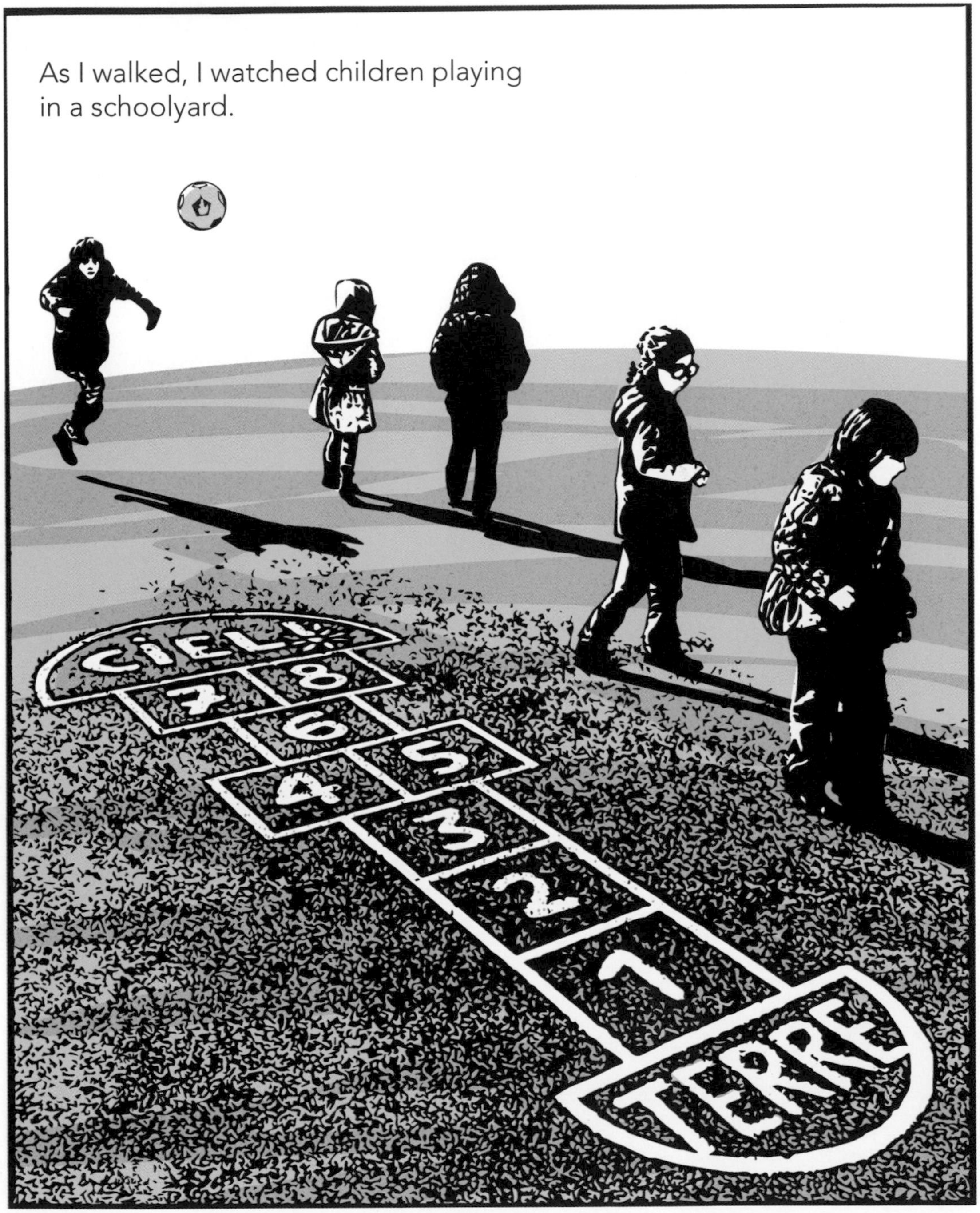
As I walked, I watched children playing
in a schoolyard.
CIEL
8
7
6
5
4
3
2
1
TERRE

Hearing them laughing
and shouting reminded me of
my grandmother's words:
You have to go to school.
I don't want you to become
a poor, ignorant woman
like me,

condemned to a life of
cleaning rich people's homes.

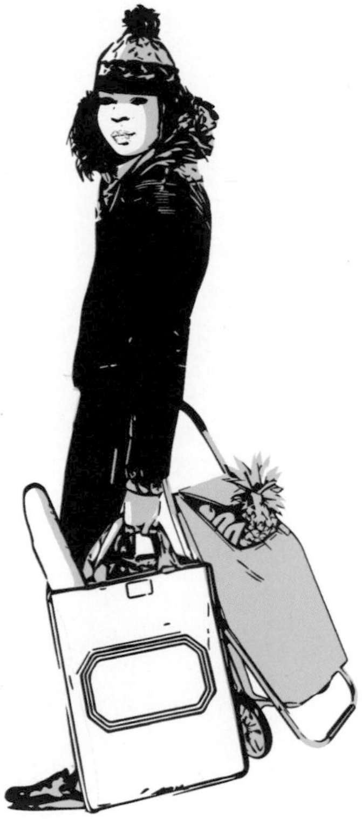

But I had to make do with leafing through Isabel's books

and any flyers and magazines that had been tossed in the wastebaskets.

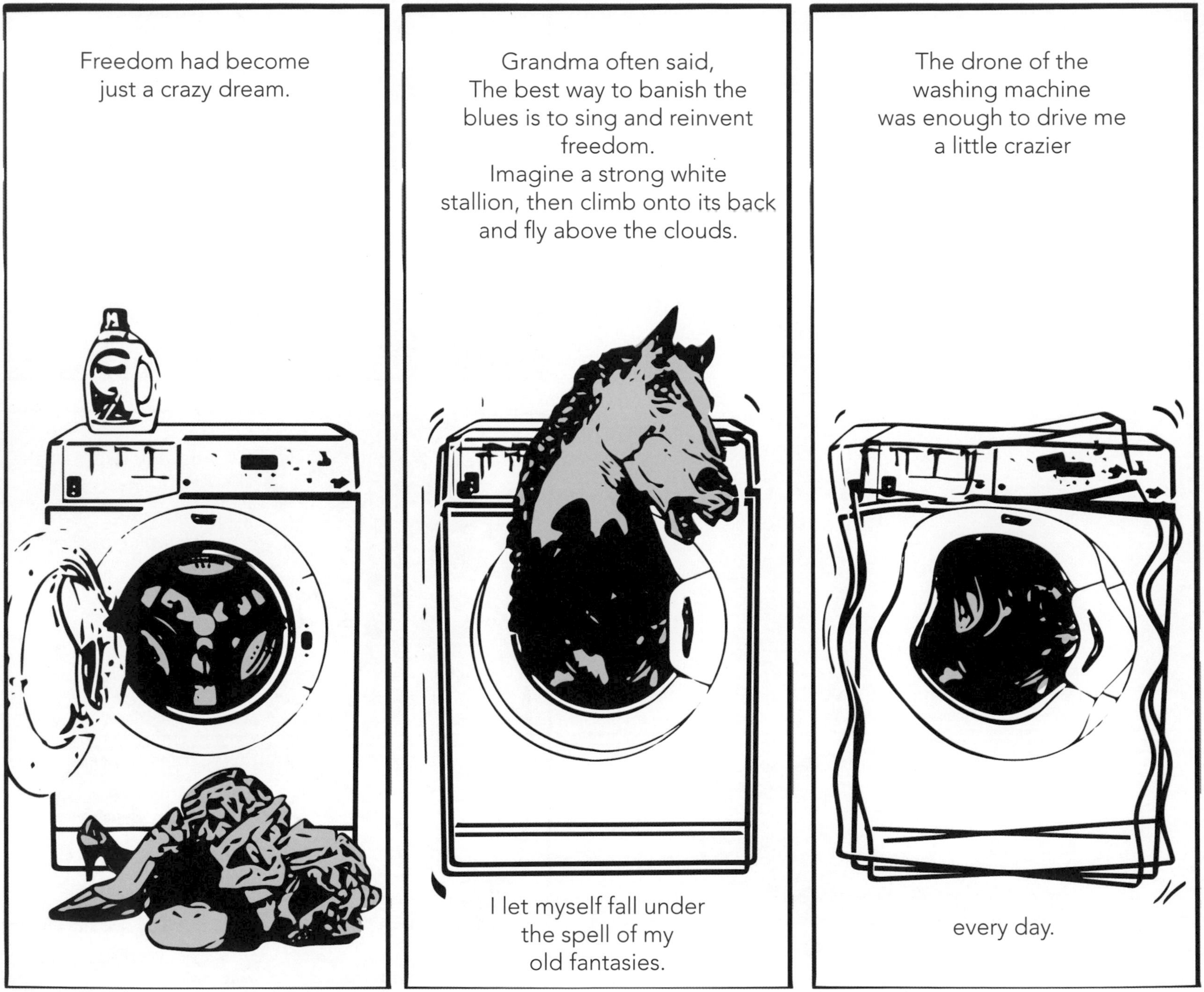
Freedom had become
just a crazy dream.
Grandma often said,
The best way to banish the
blues is to sing and reinvent
freedom.
Imagine a strong white
stallion, then climb onto its back
and fly above the clouds.
I let myself fall under
the spell of my
old fantasies.
The drone of the
washing machine
was enough to drive me
a little crazier
every day.

I was dying of boredom.

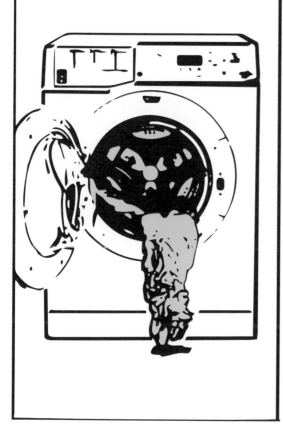

Isabel was as homesick as I was,
but at least she could
speak with her friends by video
message or text.
I managed to write to my
grandmother
and mail my letters without
being seen
whenever I could get
my hands on a postage stamp.

I told her lies
about me being happy.
I didn't want
to upset her.

Sometimes I'd receive a reply
written by the village's one teacher
because Grandma barely knew
how to read and write.

Winter

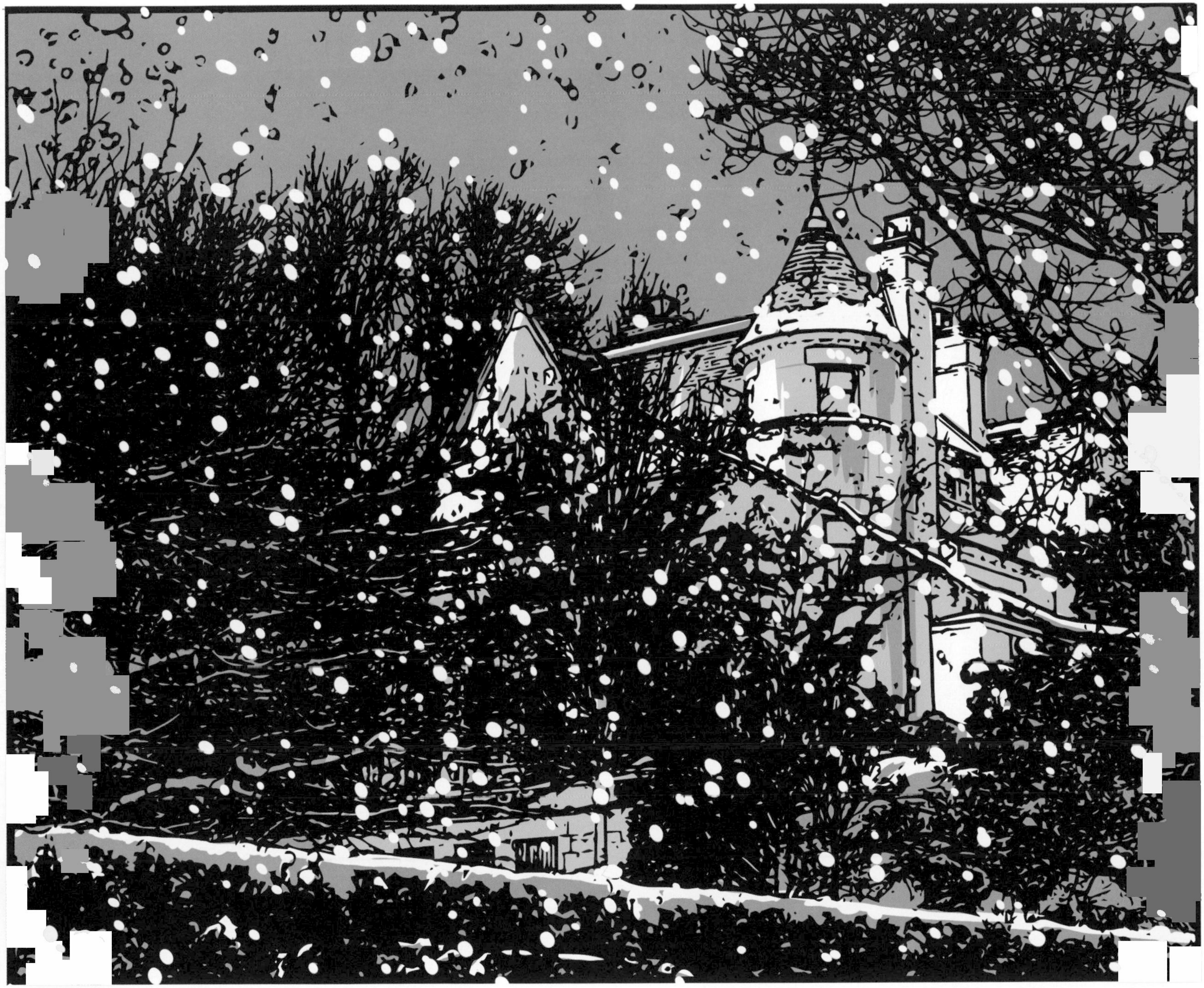

weighed me down.

The routine of daily chores

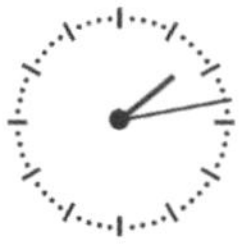

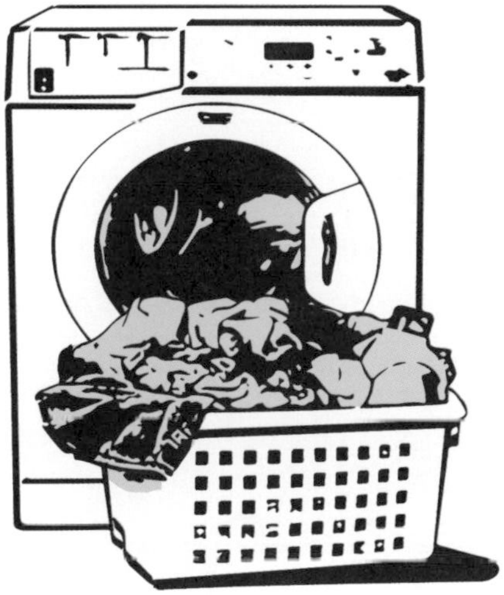

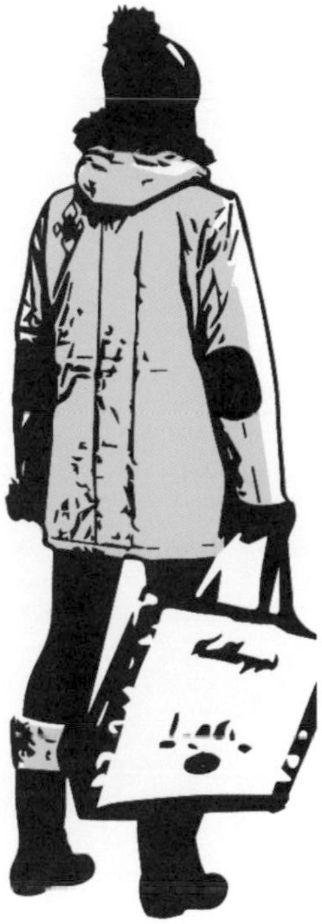

My only pleasure came from
going to the grocery store

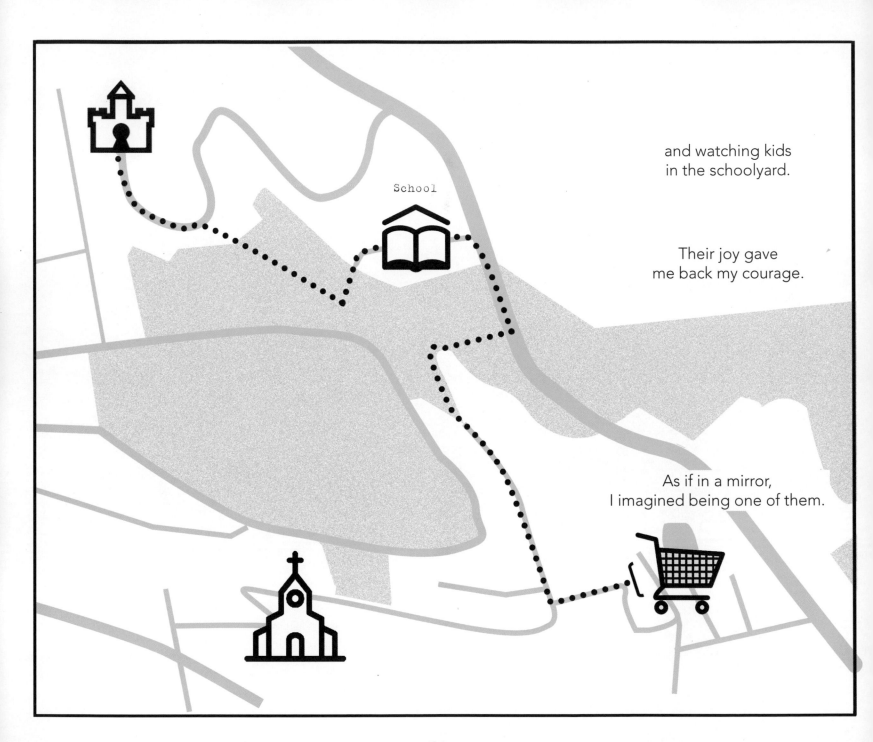

and watching kids
in the schoolyard.

Their joy gave
me back my courage.

As if in a mirror,
I imagined being one of them.

School

34

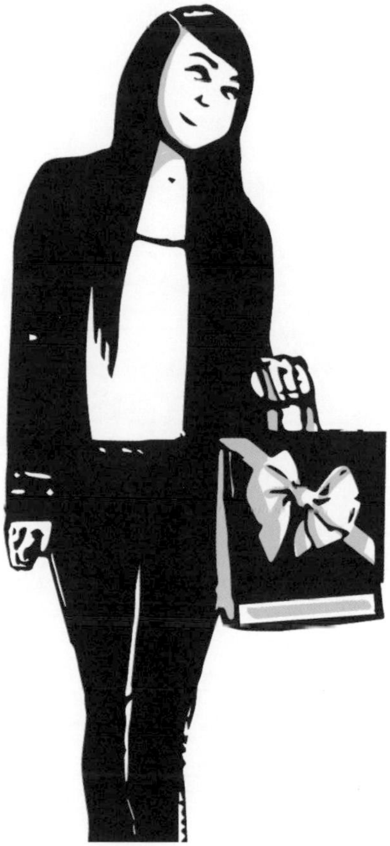

One day, Isabel gave me
a sketchbook and a box
of coloured pencils;

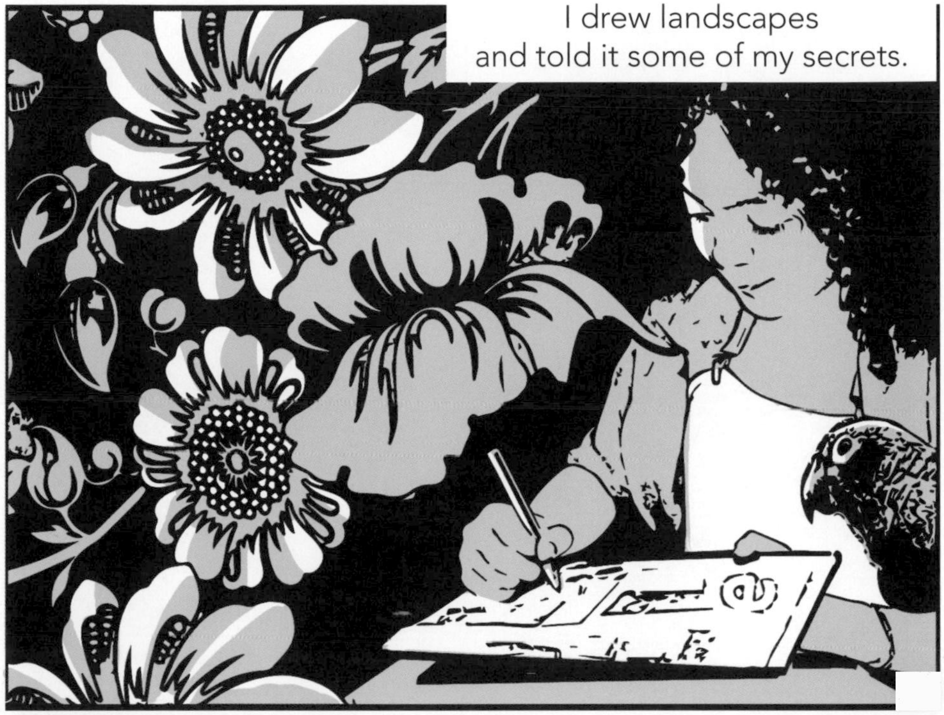
I drew landscapes
and told it some of my secrets.

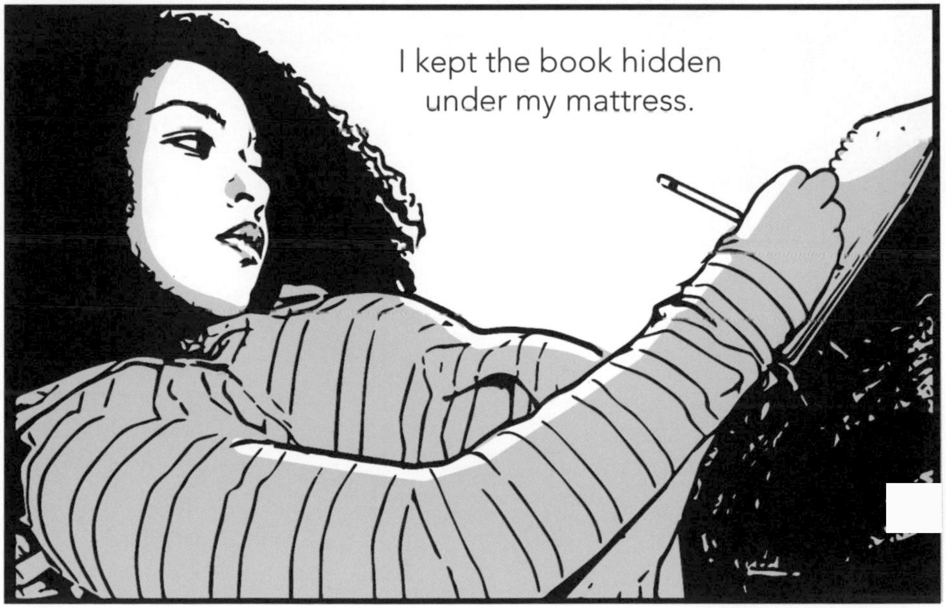
I kept the book hidden
under my mattress.

It was a morning like any other.
I thought I was home alone as
I tidied up a bedroom, but then
I heard my uncle call my name.

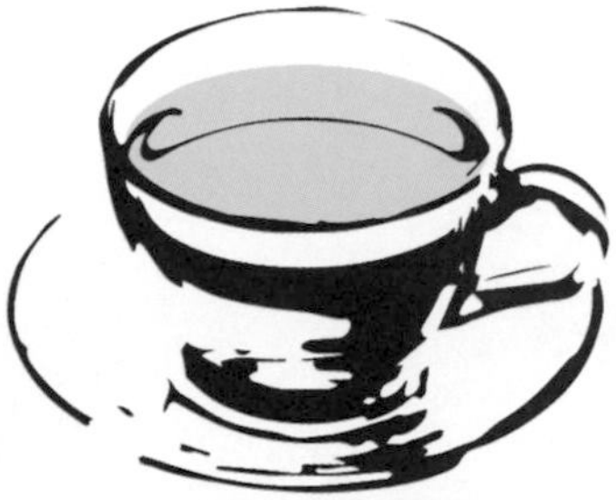

He asked me to make him some
tea and warm up two croissants.

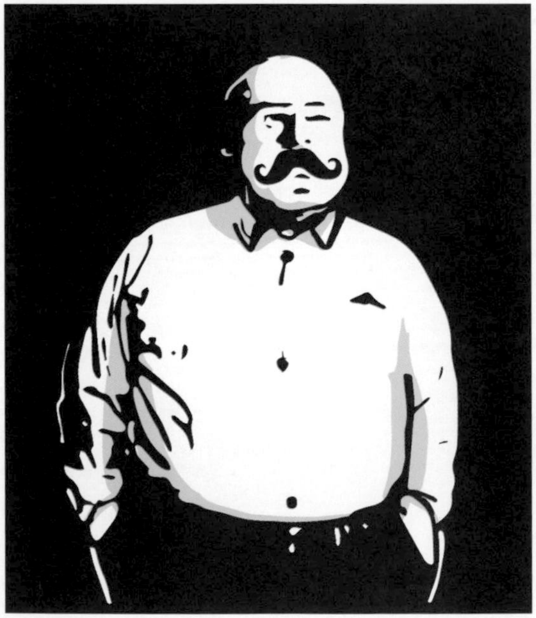

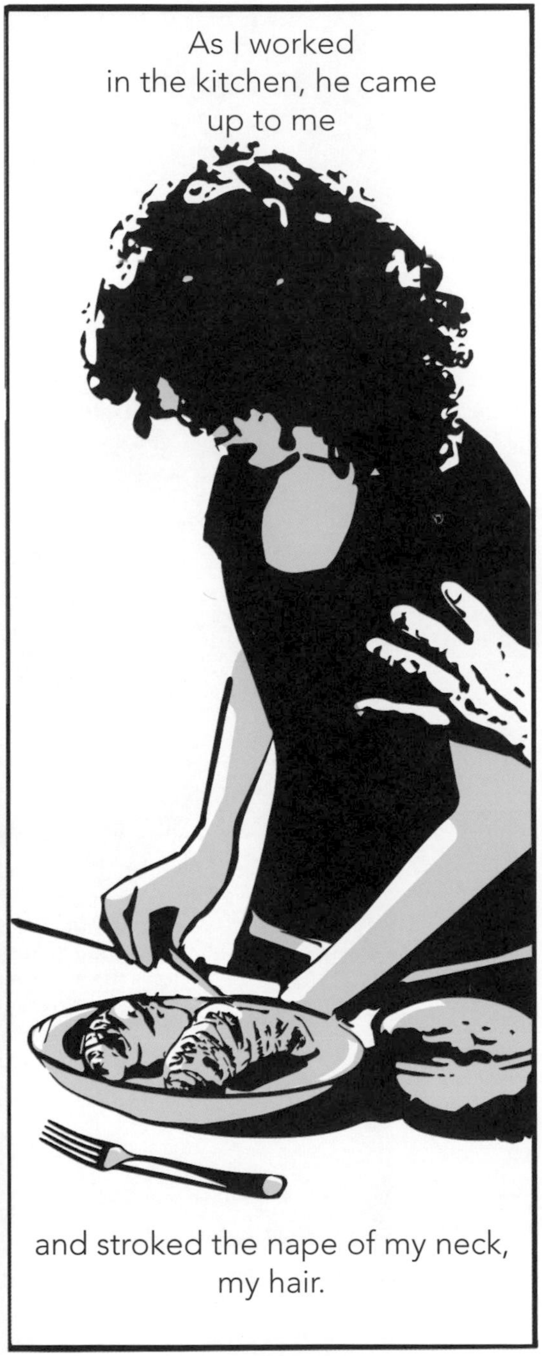
As I worked
in the kitchen, he came
up to me
and stroked the nape of my neck,
my hair.

I like your bronzed skin.

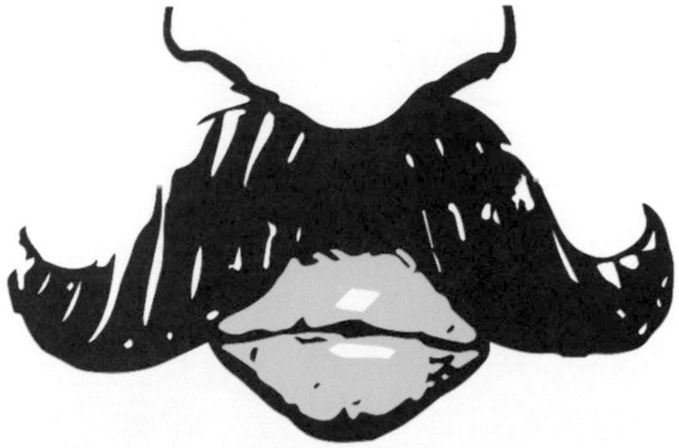

It's so warm.

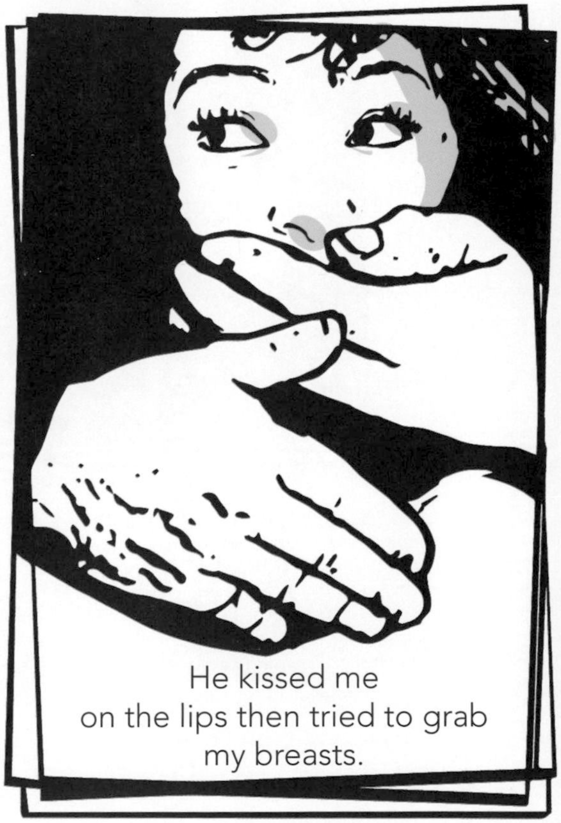
He kissed me
on the lips then tried to grab
my breasts.

I panicked and ran screaming to my bedroom. I locked the door and threw myself onto the bed, sobbing.

A few minutes later, I heard him come up the stairs. I was shaking all over. He stopped at my door and shouted,

NEVER tell anyone about this or I'll kick you out of the house! **DO YOU UNDERSTAND?**

In a feeble voice, I said,

yes

LOUDER, I CAN'T HEAR YOU!

With all my strength, I yelled,

I UNDERSTAND!

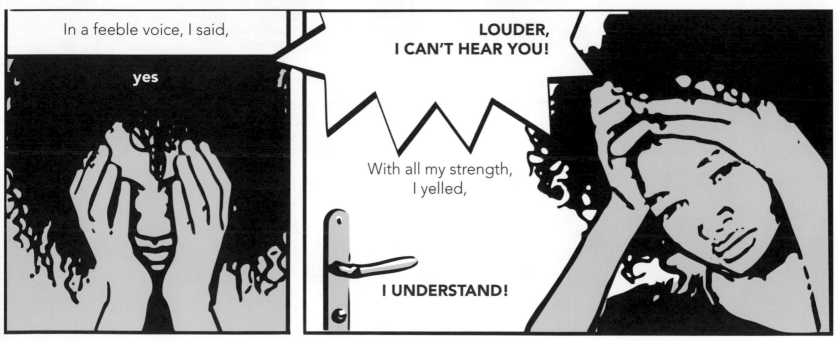

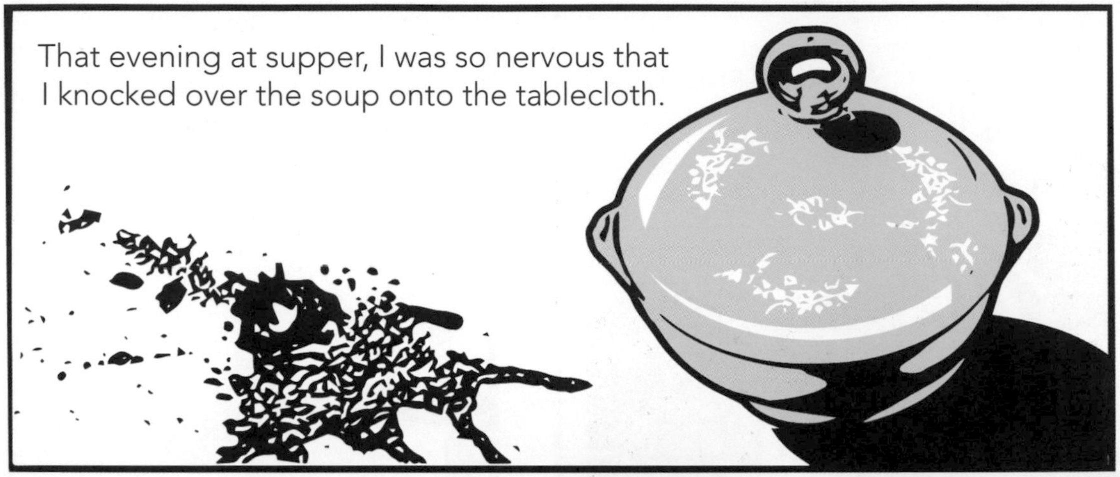
That evening at supper, I was so nervous that I knocked over the soup onto the tablecloth.

The next day and the days that followed, I found ways to get revenge.

I made trouble in small ways for all of them:

I unplugged the computers as I dusted them, broke my uncle's bottle of cognac, and did lots of other mischievous things that earned me a scolding,

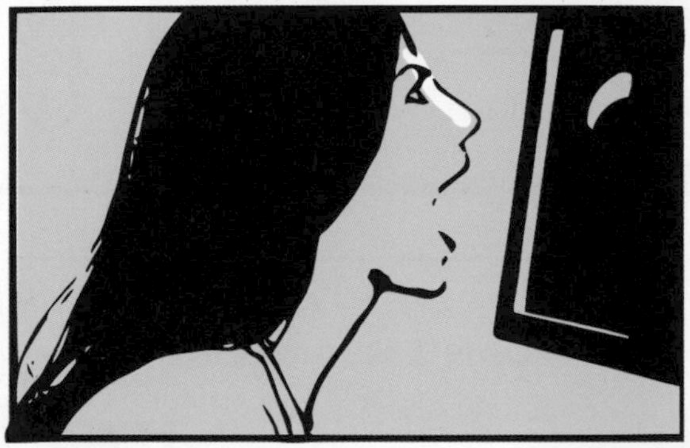

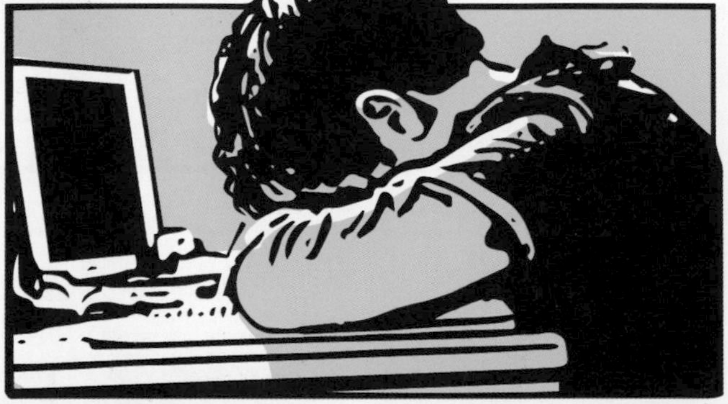

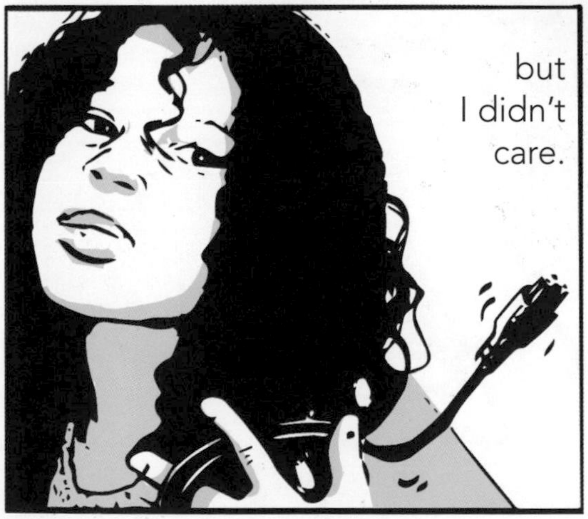
but I didn't care.

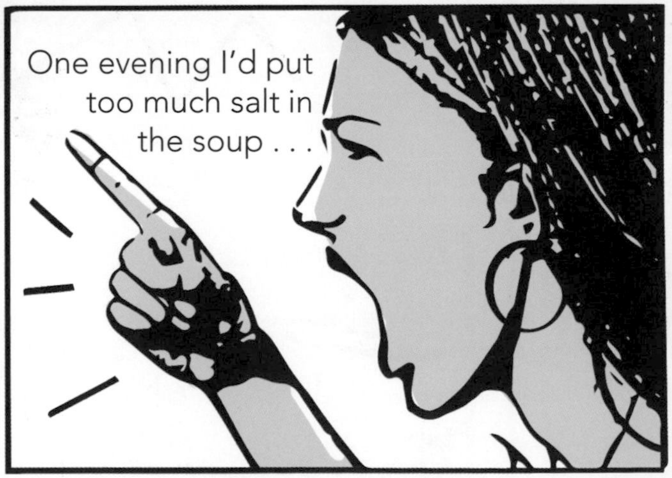
One evening I'd put too much salt in the soup . . .

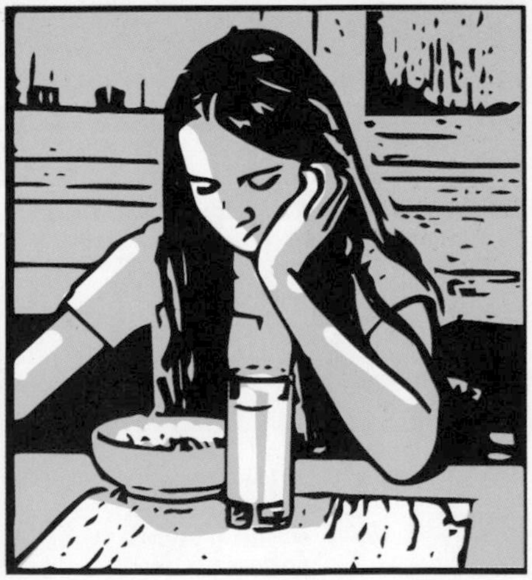

the next day I'd
overcook the meat or
spit in the stew.

It was my way
of rebelling.

Evenings got worse and worse.

While my cousins ate as a family with their parents, I served. Sometimes Isabel insisted that her mother let me eat with them, but Aunt Evoala always said no.

As for my uncle, he was often away. Even when he wasn't, he never contradicted his wife.

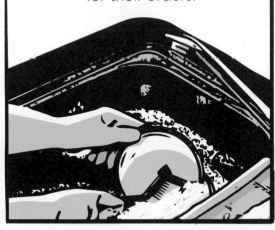

So I washed pots and pans in the kitchen and waited for their orders.

Once they finished their meal, I ate alone while the others watched TV or did their homework.

I was so jealous.

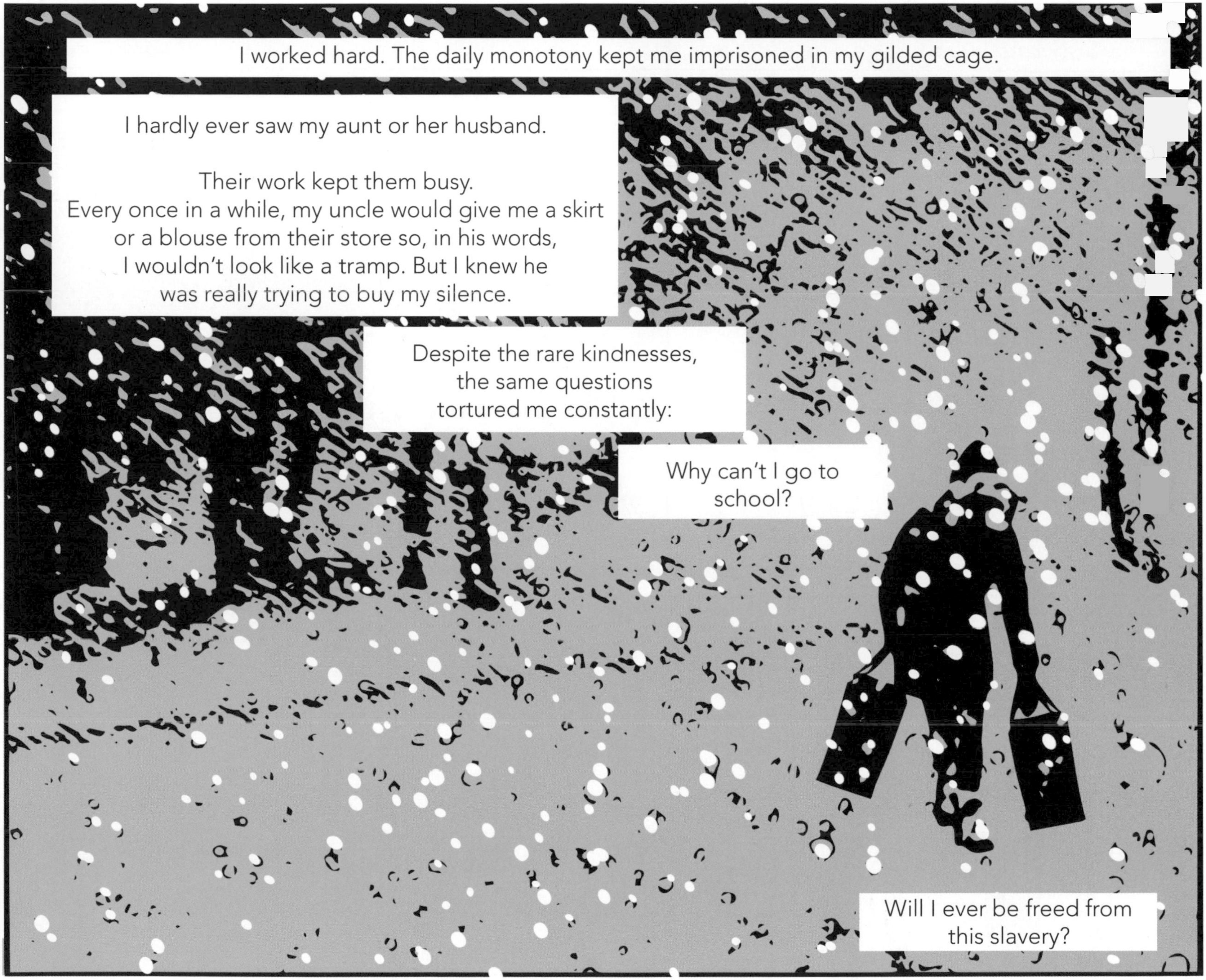
I worked hard. The daily monotony kept me imprisoned in my gilded cage.
I hardly ever saw my aunt or her husband.
Their work kept them busy.
Every once in a while, my uncle would give me a skirt or a blouse from their store so, in his words, I wouldn't look like a tramp. But I knew he was really trying to buy my silence.
Despite the rare kindnesses, the same questions tortured me constantly:
Why can't I go to school?
Will I ever be freed from this slavery?

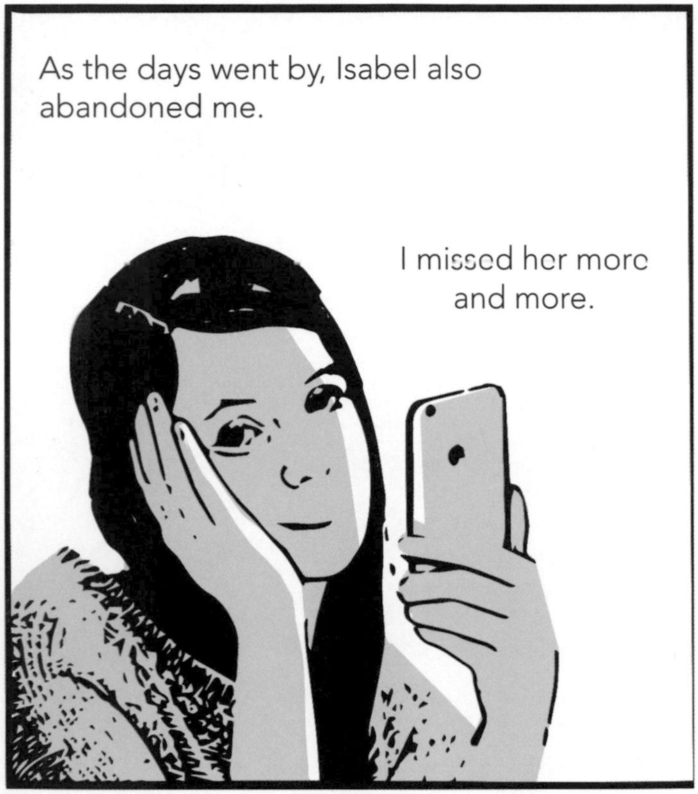
As the days went by, Isabel also abandoned me.
I missed her more and more.

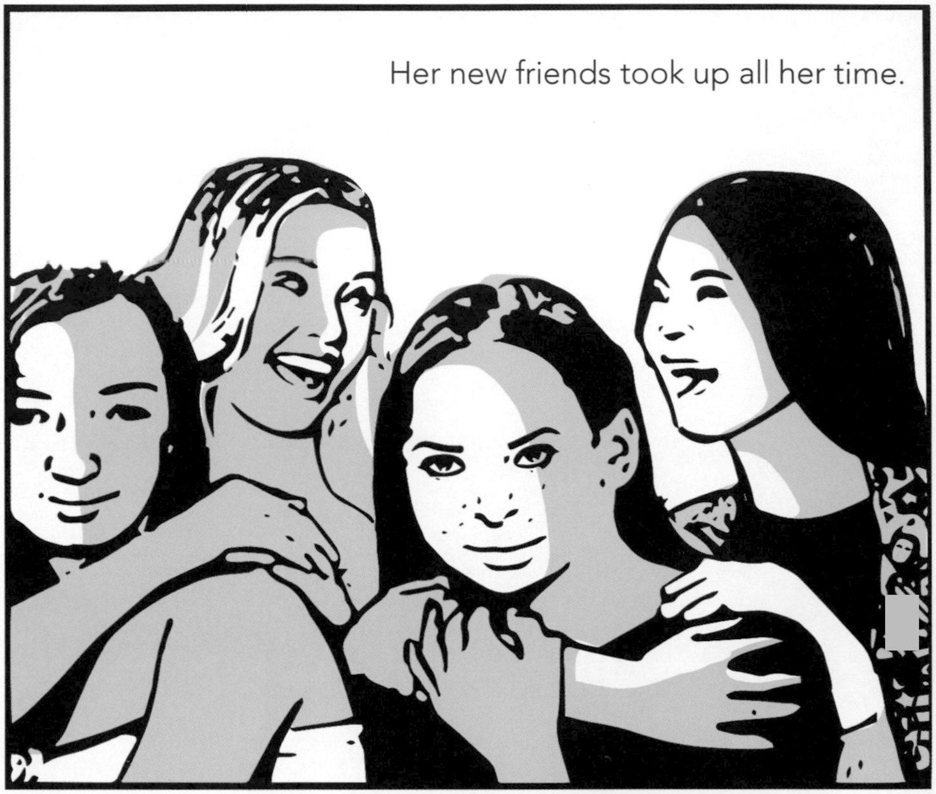
Her new friends took up all her time.

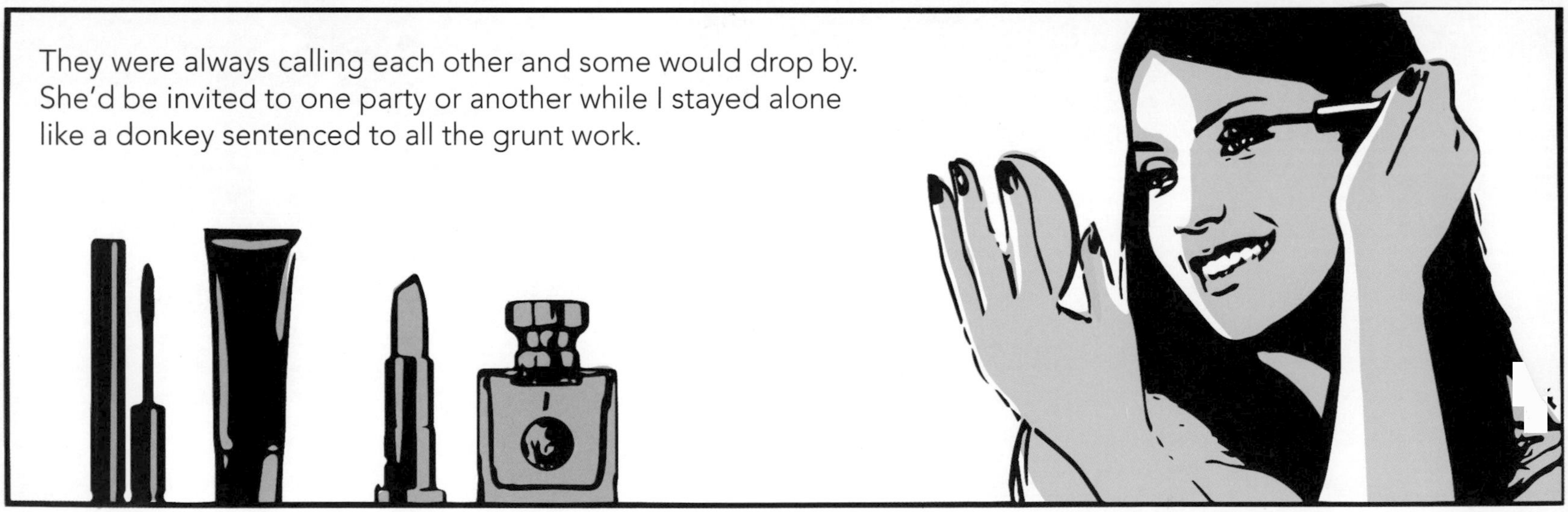
They were always calling each other and some would drop by. She'd be invited to one party or another while I stayed alone like a donkey sentenced to all the grunt work.

If, as they say, wealth from hard work
really does grow over time,
I should end up a millionaire.

Being invisible hurt
like a red hot iron
scorching my skin.

Spring

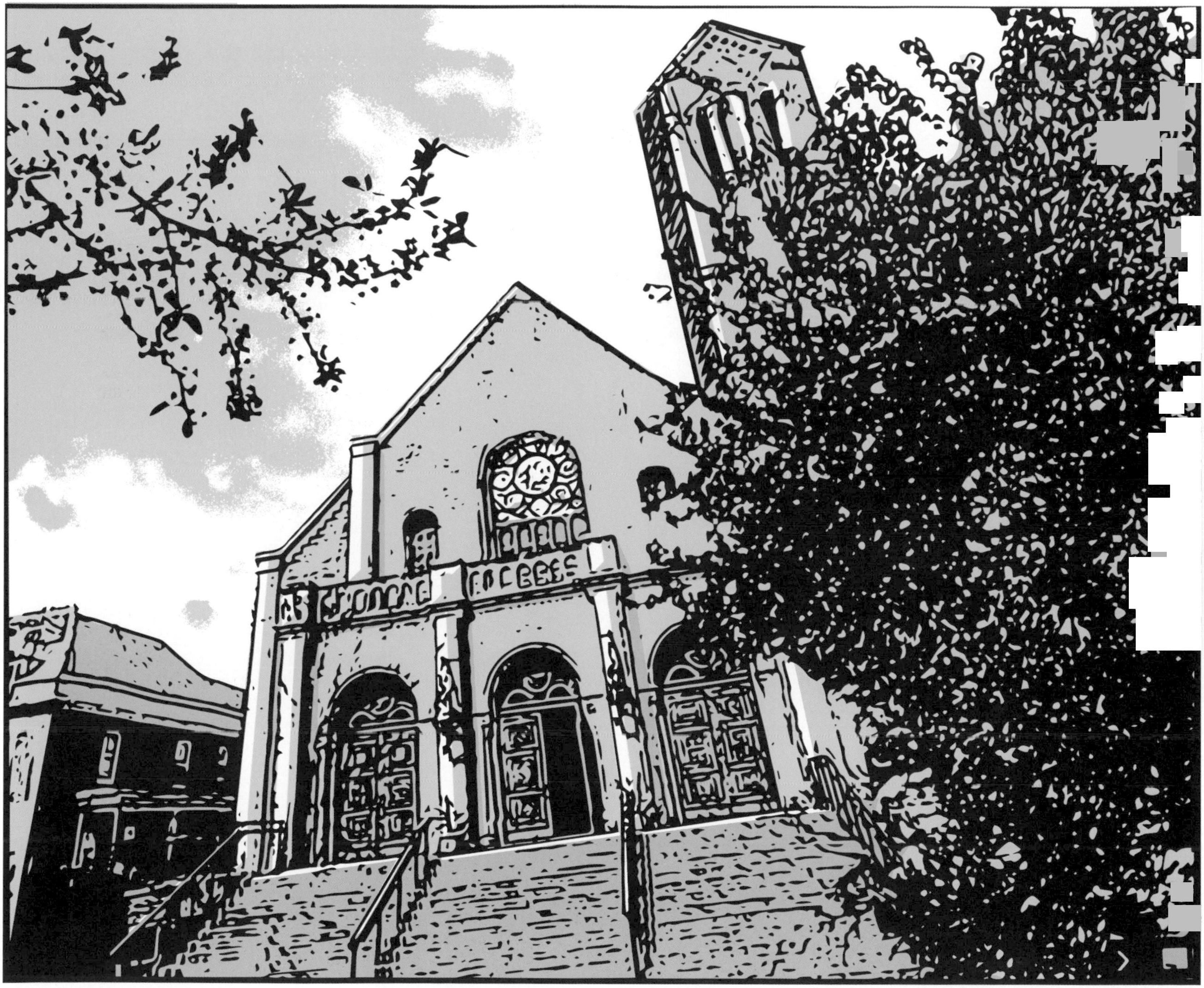

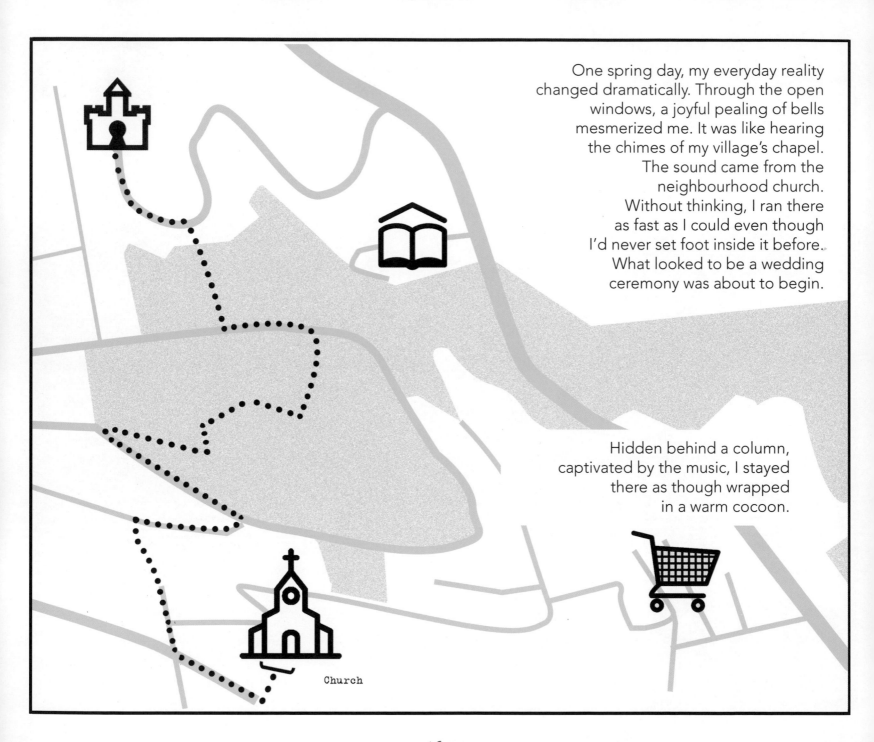

One spring day, my everyday reality changed dramatically. Through the open windows, a joyful pealing of bells mesmerized me. It was like hearing the chimes of my village's chapel. The sound came from the neighbourhood church. Without thinking, I ran there as fast as I could even though I'd never set foot inside it before. What looked to be a wedding ceremony was about to begin.

Hidden behind a column, captivated by the music, I stayed there as though wrapped in a warm cocoon.

Church

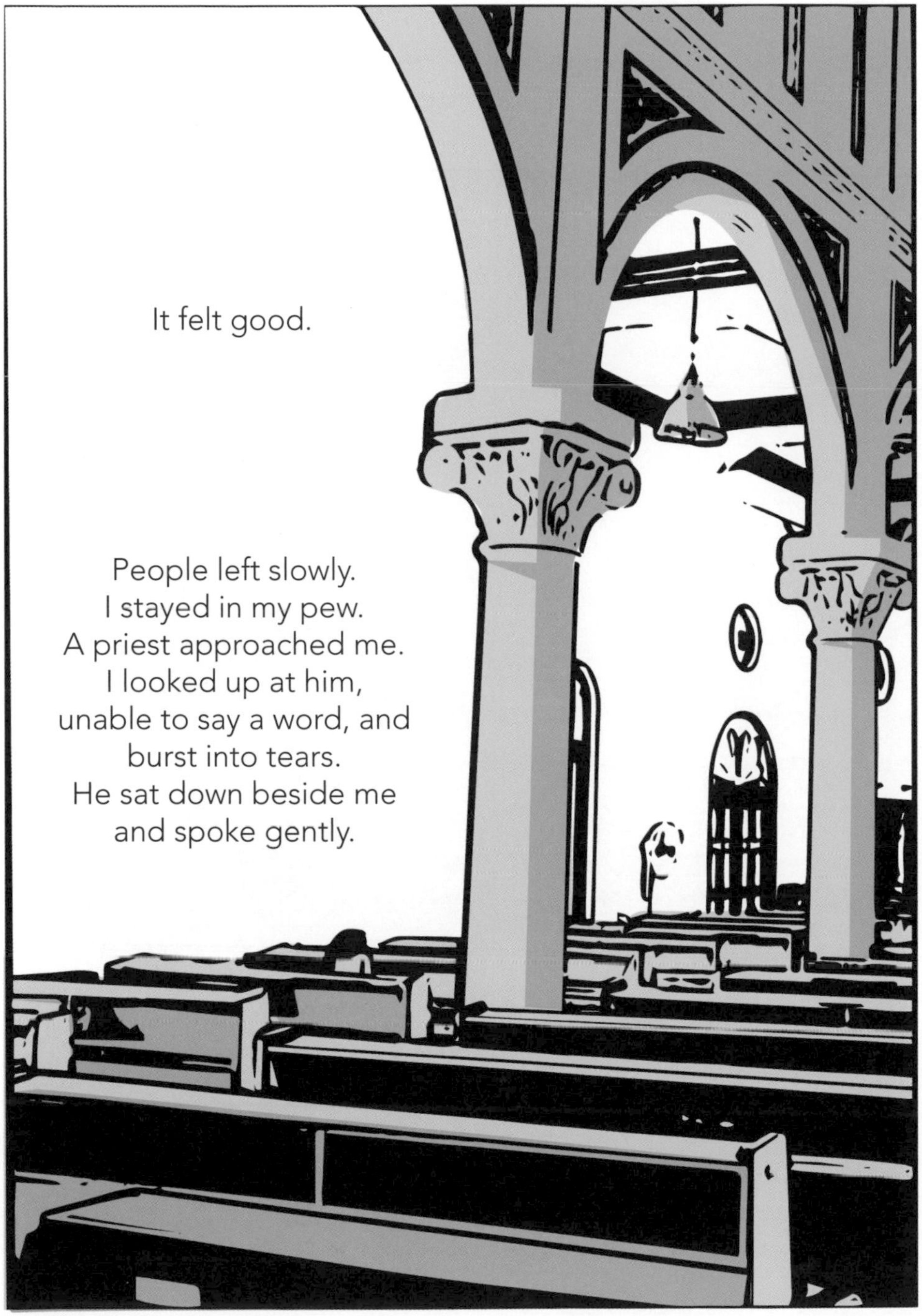
It felt good.
People left slowly. I stayed in my pew. A priest approached me. I looked up at him, unable to say a word, and burst into tears. He sat down beside me and spoke gently.

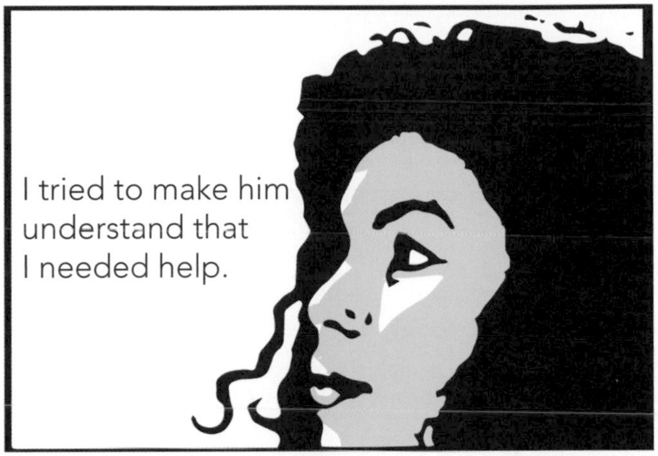
I tried to make him understand that I needed help.

Seeing how hard it was for me to express myself, he answered in Spanish.

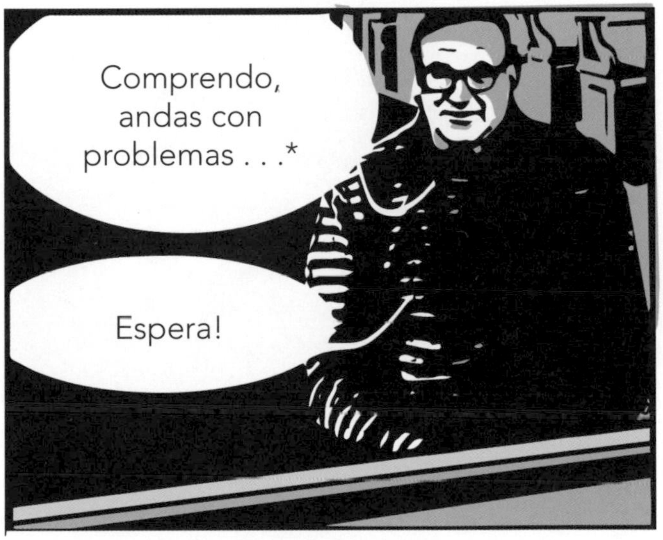
Comprendo, andas con problemas . . .*
Espera!

I felt a twinge of fear, but delight and trust too.

*I understand. You need help . . . Wait here!

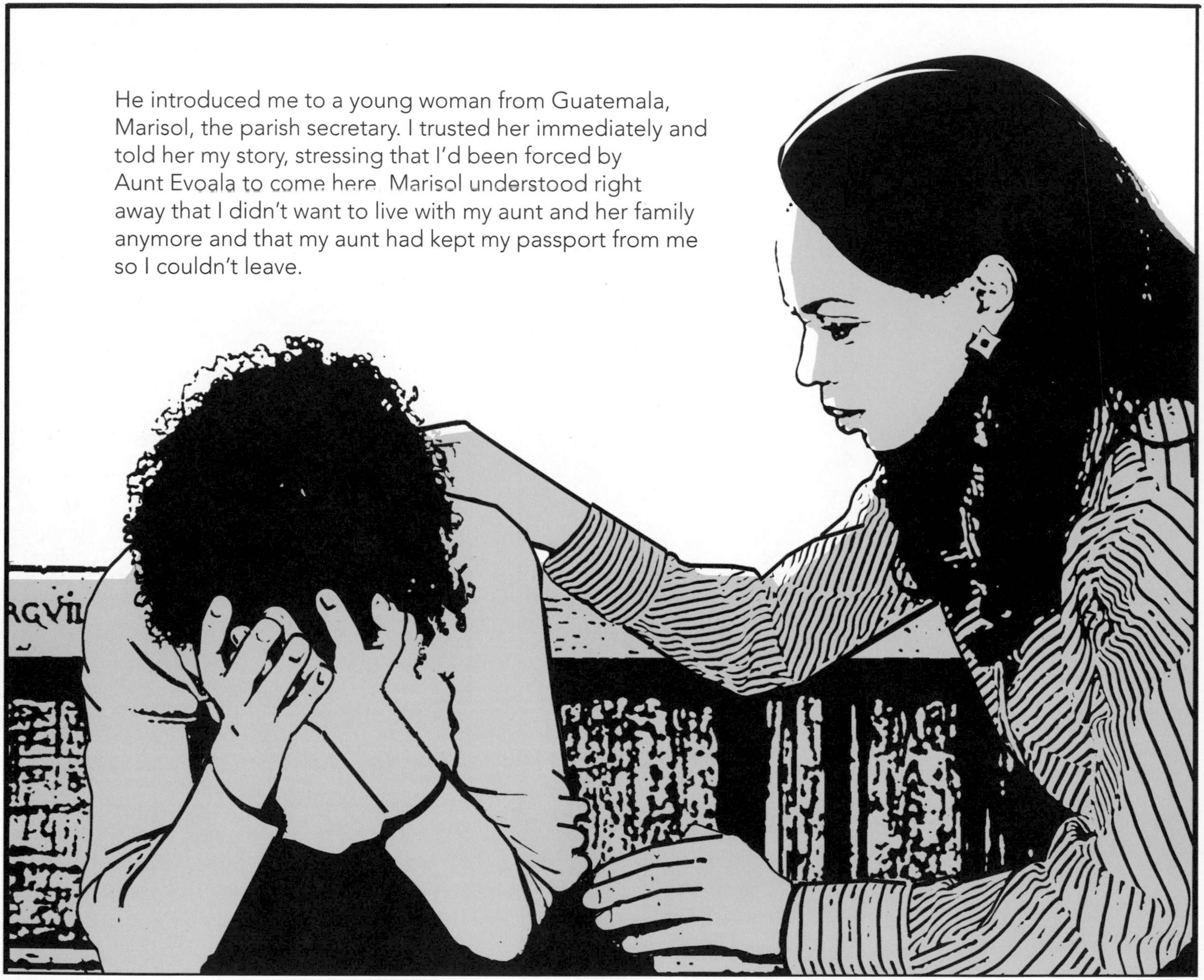
He introduced me to a young woman from Guatemala, Marisol, the parish secretary. I trusted her immediately and told her my story, stressing that I'd been forced by Aunt Evoala to come here. Marisol understood right away that I didn't want to live with my aunt and her family anymore and that my aunt had kept my passport from me so I couldn't leave.

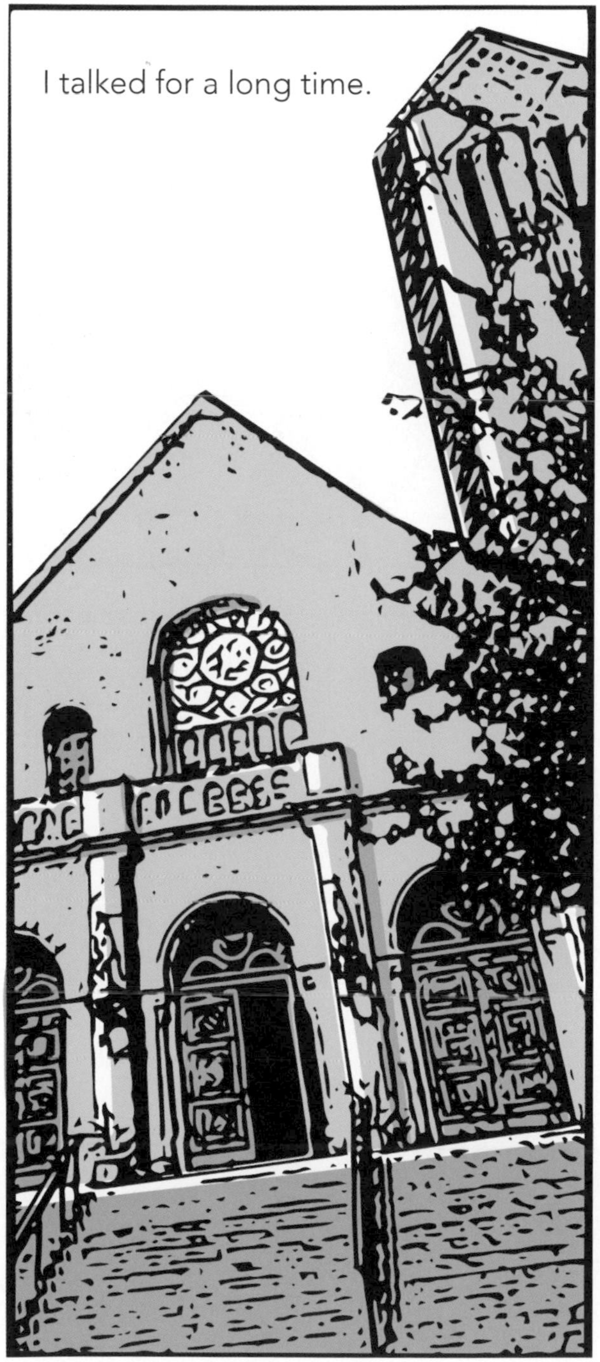
I talked for a long time.

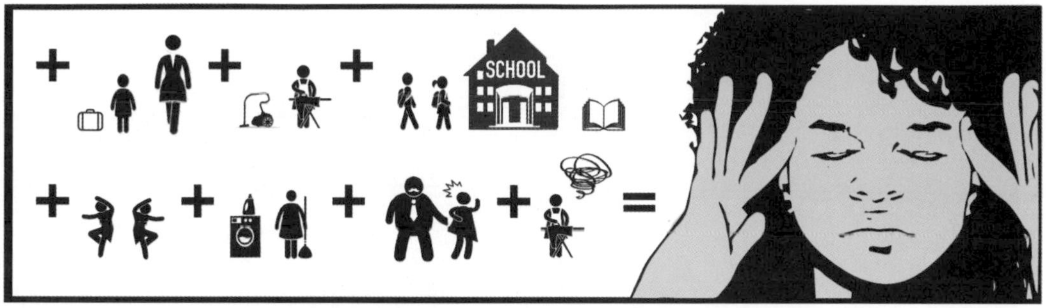
SCHOOL

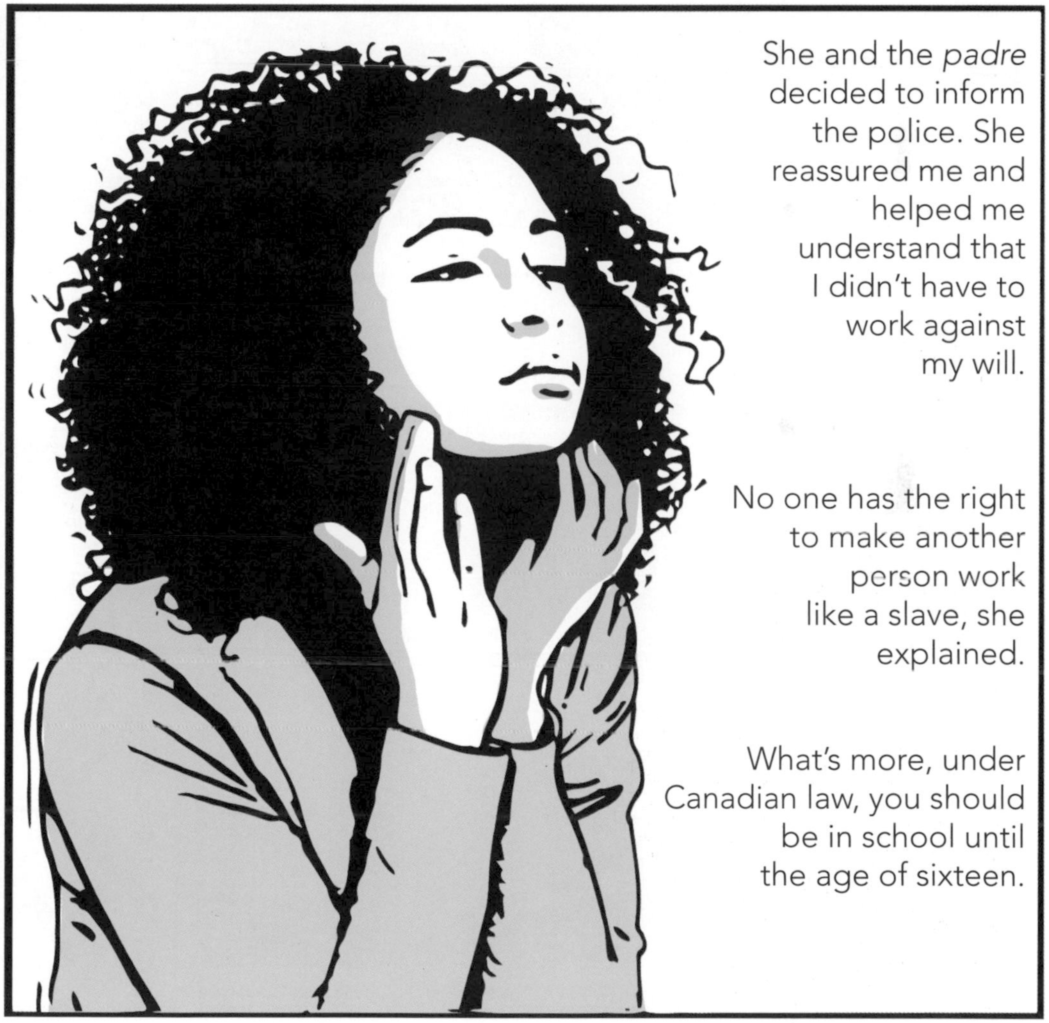
She and the *padre* decided to inform the police. She reassured me and helped me understand that I didn't have to work against my will.
No one has the right to make another person work like a slave, she explained.
What's more, under Canadian law, you should be in school until the age of sixteen.

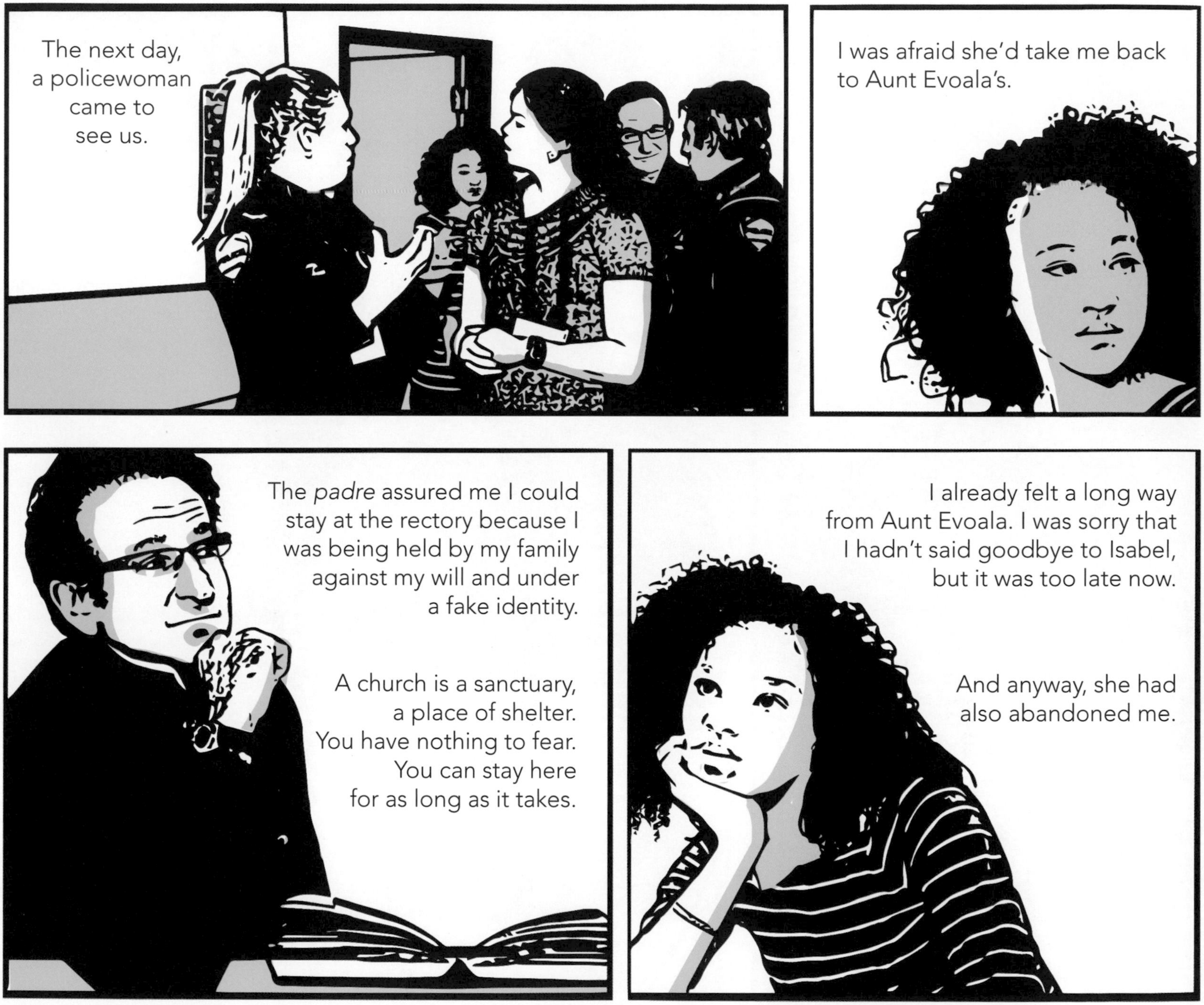
The next day, a policewoman came to see us.
I was afraid she'd take me back to Aunt Evoala's.
The *padre* assured me I could stay at the rectory because I was being held by my family against my will and under a fake identity.
A church is a sanctuary, a place of shelter. You have nothing to fear. You can stay here for as long as it takes.
I already felt a long way from Aunt Evoala. I was sorry that I hadn't said goodbye to Isabel, but it was too late now.
And anyway, she had also abandoned me.

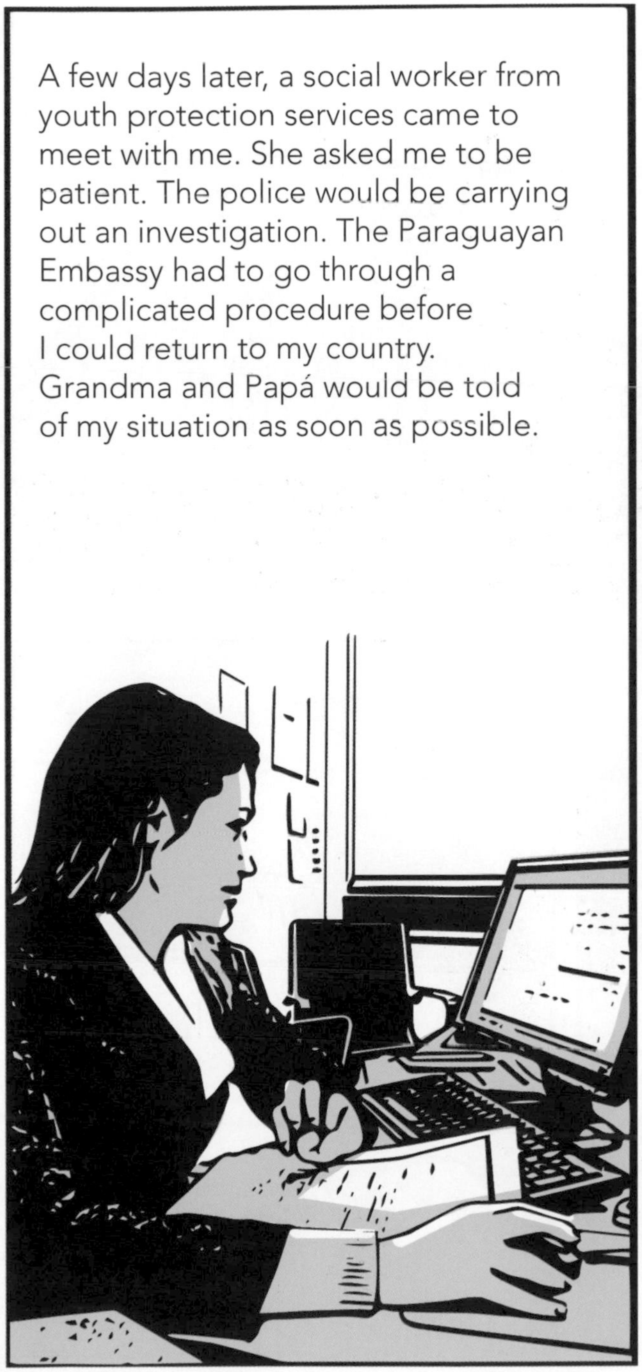
A few days later, a social worker from youth protection services came to meet with me. She asked me to be patient. The police would be carrying out an investigation. The Paraguayan Embassy had to go through a complicated procedure before I could return to my country. Grandma and Papá would be told of my situation as soon as possible.

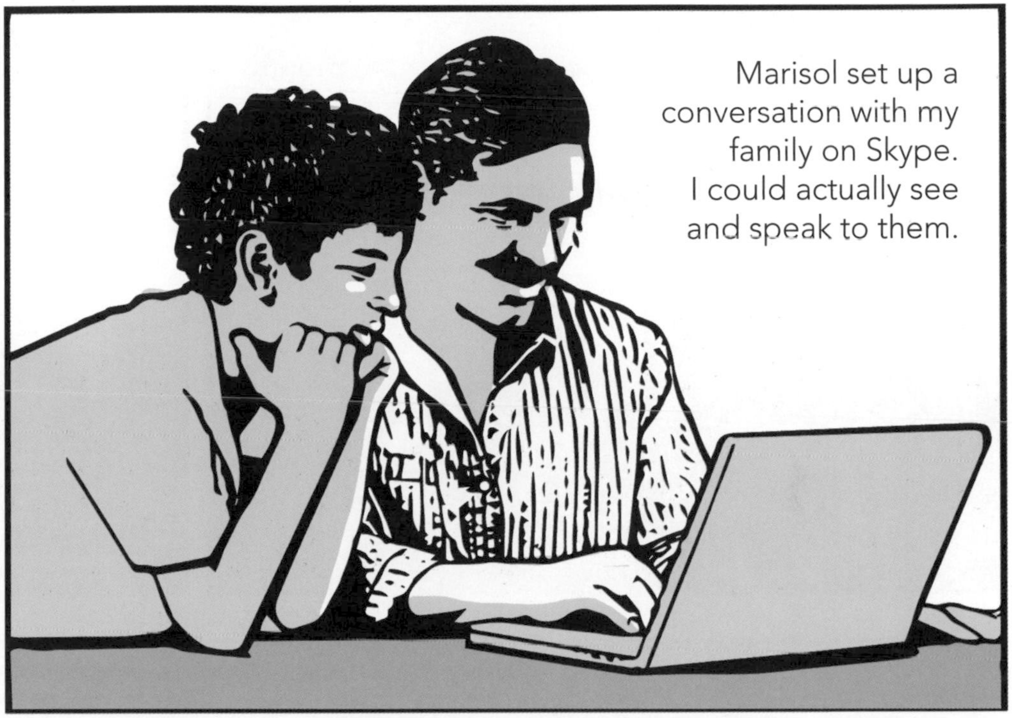
Marisol set up a conversation with my family on Skype. I could actually see and speak to them.

They'd gone to the village post office, where there's a computer.

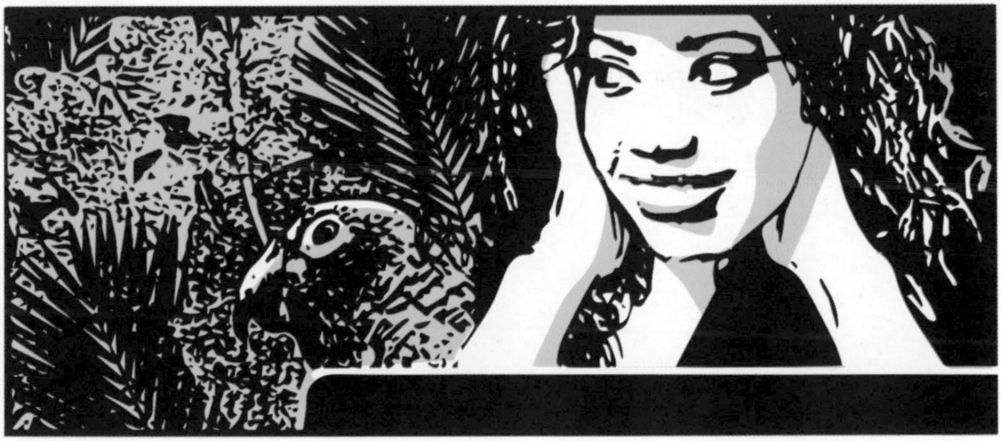

We were all wild with joy knowing we'd be seeing one another again soon, after a long year of being apart.

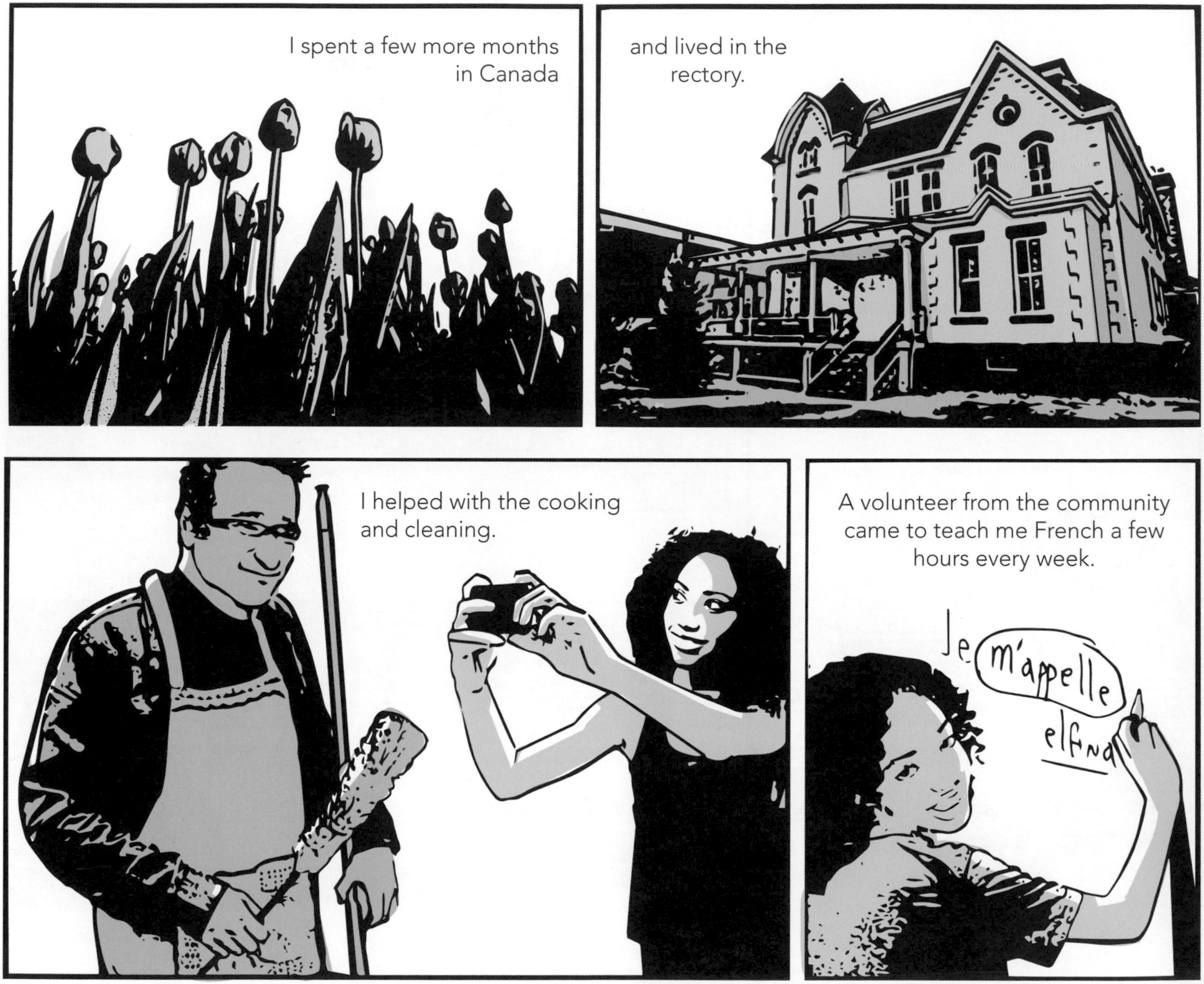
I spent a few more months in Canada
and lived in the rectory.
I helped with the cooking and cleaning.
A volunteer from the community came to teach me French a few hours every week.
Je m'appelle

I told investigators
my story several times as I waited
for the police to resolve the issues
with Aunt Evoala's family.

The police department and
immigration and border services
agents wanted to know
everything about my life with the
family since I'd left my village.

One day, we were told that my aunt's
whole family had been deported to my
country and banned from returning to
Canada. They were charged
with unlawfully confining me. Later,
I learned that millions of other girls like
me experience the same situation all
around the world.

Soon afterwards, the *padre* gave me
a new passport.
I cried with joy.

A few days later,
I received a
plane ticket
thanks
to donations
from the *padre*'s
friends.

Marisol and a Canadian border services agent
took me to the airport. I was sorry to
say goodbye, but thrilled to be free.
Finally, I would see my family again
even though I was afraid Aunt
Evoala might cause new problems for me.

Summer

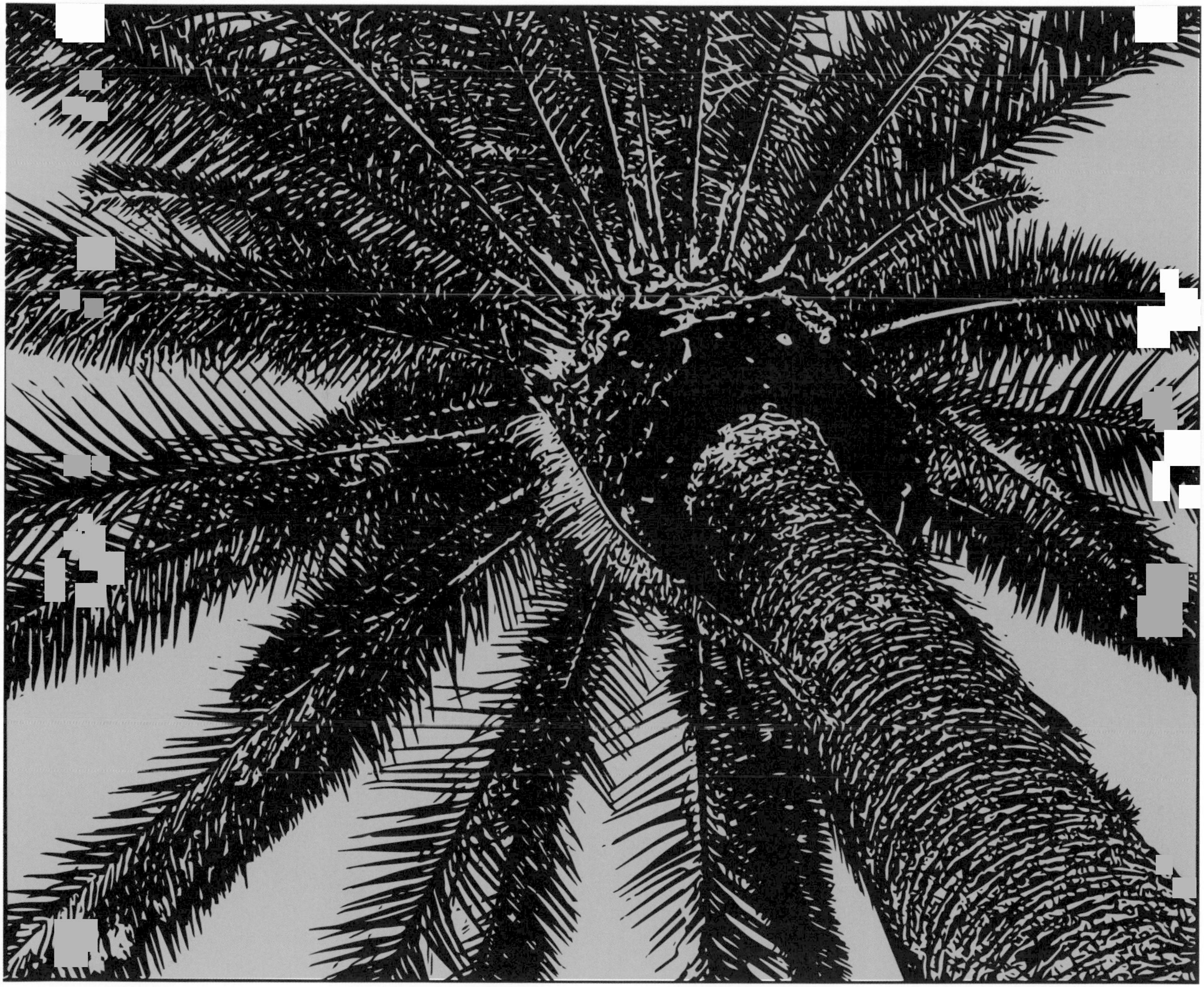

When I arrived in the capital,
Papá was waiting for me at the airport. He cried as much as I did,
saying over and over that he'd always keep me with him.

He was so sorry for letting me go with Aunt Evoala.

"I made a big mistake, but I wanted
you to be able to study in a big city school.
She promised to look after you.

But she lied. Now you'll return
to school here."

On the way home, he talked non-stop.

To my delight, he told me he'd
decided to stay home and cultivate a market garden.
He would sell the fruits and vegetables in the city.

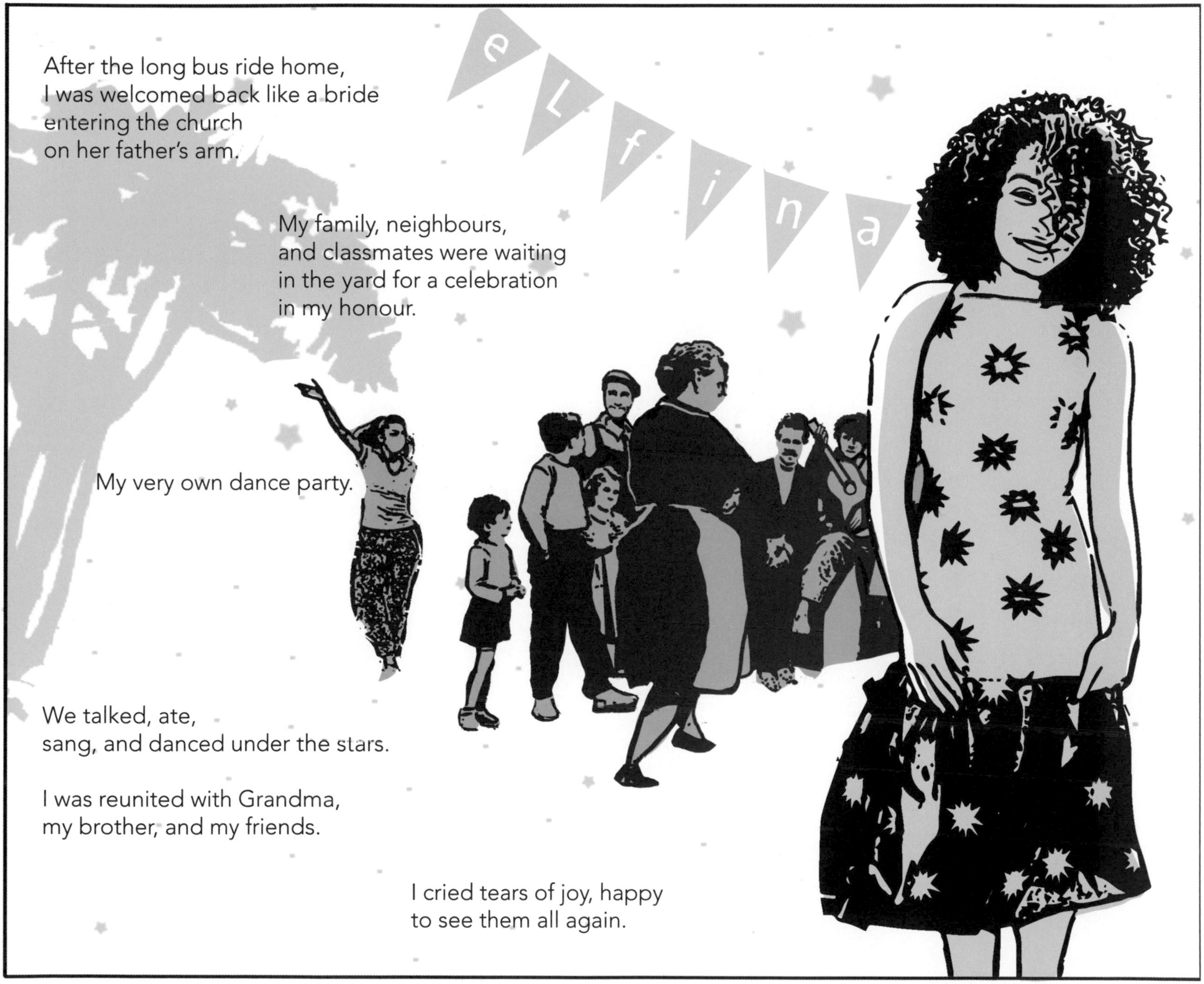
elfina

After the long bus ride home,
I was welcomed back like a bride
entering the church
on her father's arm.

My family, neighbours,
and classmates were waiting
in the yard for a celebration
in my honour.

My very own dance party.

We talked, ate,
sang, and danced under the stars.

I was reunited with Grandma,
my brother, and my friends.

I cried tears of joy, happy
to see them all again.

Epilogue

A few weeks after I got back,
I was thrilled to be able to go back to school.
As the months went by, I kept in regular touch
with the *padre* and Marisol. They promised
to help me continue my studies as soon as
I graduate from the village school. Thanks to the *padre*,
I plan to apply for scholarships
to go to university because I want to become
a doctor and maybe even go back to Canada
to study. But I still have a lot of schooling to do here
before I reach that stage.

Like all young people
my age,
I now have the right
to dream.

Further Reading

Forced child labour is unacceptable.

Numbers talk

Elfina's tale doesn't tell the whole story. Her experience as shown in these few pages is only an illustration, a snapshot, of what millions of children and teens go through worldwide. Data from the International Labour Organization (ILO) is extremely troubling.[1] Since the year 2000, the number of children in difficult circumstances has dropped from 246 million to 168 million, but 85 million still live in dangerous situations because of the type of employment they are involved in. The ILO estimates that there are nearly 21 million youth victims of forced labour: 11.4 million young women and girls and 9.5 million young men and boys. Among these young people, 4.5 million are exploited sexually. Children work in all sectors of the economy, but especially in agriculture (98 million), shops, mines, industries, and domestic labour like Elfina. In the global economy, forced child labour produces 150 billion dollars in illegal profits each year.

Why does this tragedy still happen?

The first and foremost factor is poverty. Large populations remain destitute because businesses exploit their labour at low or sometimes no wages, except for a bit of food and shelter. Take the case of cocoa or coffee plantations. By using child labour (for pruning, harvesting, etc.), plantations and importers of the commodities are able to make huge profits.

---

1   www.ilo.org/global/topics/forced-labour/lang--en/index.htm

The second factor is a lack of access to education. In many countries, millions of children and teens cannot go to school due to non-existent or unenforced laws and policies. This is a violation of children's rights, as education should be a right respected worldwide. All nations should ensure free access to primary and secondary education for both girls and boys. In certain parts of the world, school is more easily accessible for boys than girls; often girls are deprived of an education altogether.

Fundamental solutions

The 1989 Convention on the Rights of the Child is clear.[2] Children have rights and freedoms. Children are entitled to decent living conditions, which means respect for all their rights, including the right to housing, education, food, and freedom from child labour.

The fight against poverty should be a goal for every country in the world.

André Jacob

ANDRÉ JACOB is a former professor and has been a guest lecturer on immigration, racism and international development around the world. He is also a professional visual artist and vice-chairman of Artists for Peace. André lives in Mascouche, Québec.

CHRISTINE DELEZENNE is a graphic designer and an illustrator. She integrates various elements in her art — drawings, textures, collages and photos. She lives in Switzerland.

---

2   www.humanium.org/en/convention

Resources:

Several organizations work to promote children's rights, including UNICEF,[3] Alliance 8.7[4] (which brings together several countries committed to banning and eliminating the worst forms of child labour, including the recruitment and use of child soldiers), and Red Card to Child Labour.[5]

Behnke, Alison Marie. *Up for Sale: Human Trafficking and Modern Slavery*. Minnesota: Lerner, 2014.

Collins, Tara, et al., eds. *Rights of the Child: Proceedings of the International Conference, Ottawa 2007*. Montreal: Wilson & Lafleur, 2008.

Hall, Shyima. *Hidden Girl: The True Story of a Modern Day Child Slave*. New York: Simon & Schuster Books for Young Readers, 2014.

Human Rights Watch. *Human Rights Watch Submission to the UN Working Group on Discrimination Against Women in Law and Practice*. Women and Girls Deprived of Liberty, September 2018. New York: Human Rights Watch, 2018.

Moccia, Patricia, ed. *The State of the World's Children*. Special Edition: Celebrating 20 Years of the Convention on the Rights of the Child. New York: UNICEF, 2009.

UNICEF. *The State of the World's Children 2017: Children in a digital world*. New York: UNICEF, 2017.

Yousafzai, Malala. *I am Malala: The Girl Who Stood Up for Education and was Shot by the Taliban*. Boston: Little, Brown and Company, 2013.

---

3   www.unicef.ca/en?adid=110415322138
4   www.alliance87.org
5   www.ilo.org/ipec/Campaignandadvocacy/RedCardtoChildLabour/lang--en/index.htm

English edition © James Lorimer & Company, 2019

Originally published in French as *Les quatre saisons d'Elfina* by les Éditions de l'Isatis.
French edition © André Jacob, Christine Delezenne et les Éditions de l'Isatis, 2017

Published in Canada in 2019. Published in the United States in 2019.

James Lorimer & Company Ltd., Publishers acknowledges funding support from the Ontario Arts Council (OAC), an agency of the Government of Ontario. We acknowledge the support of the Canada Council for the Arts, which last year invested $153 million to bring the arts to Canadians throughout the country. This project has been made possible with the support of Ontario Creates. We acknowledge the support of the Government of Canada through the National Translation Program for Book Publishing, an initiative of the *Roadmap for Canada's Official Languages 2013-2019: Education, Immigration, Communities*, for our translation activities.

Cover design: Éditions de l'Isatis
Cover image: Christine Delezenne

Library and Archives Canada Cataloguing in Publication

Jacob, André
[Quatre saisons d'Elfina. English]
    The courage of Elfina / André Jacob ; illustrated by Christine Delezenne ; translated by Susan Ouriou.

Translation of: Les quatre saisons d'Elfina.
Includes bibliographical references.
ISBN 978-1-4594-1419-8 (hardcover)

    1. Graphic novels. I. Ouriou, Susan, translator II. Delezenne, Christine, 1965-, illustrator III. Title. VI. Title: Quatre saisons d'Elfina. English

PN6733.J32Q3813 2019   j741.5'971   C2018-905303-8

Published by:
James Lorimer & Company Ltd., Publishers
117 Peter Street, Suite 304
Toronto, ON, Canada
M5V 0M3
www.lorimer.ca

Distributed in Canada by:
Formac Lorimer Books
5502 Atlantic Street
Halifax, NS, Canada
B3H 1G4

Distributed in the US by:
Lerner Publisher Services
1251 Washington Ave. N.
Minneapolis, MN, USA
55401
www.lernerbooks.com

Printed and bound in China.

Manufactured by Everbest Printing

Job # 815149

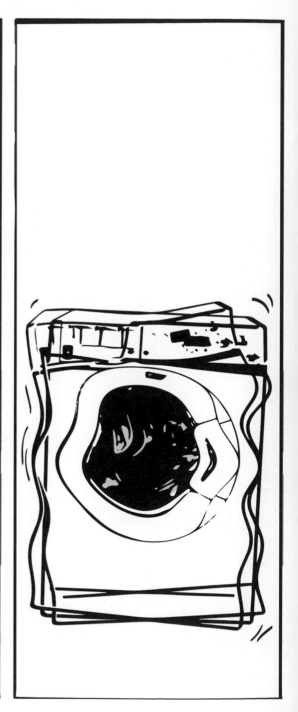